PHILLIS WHEATLEY

YOUNG REVOLUTIONARY POET

Written by
Kathryn Kilby Borland and
Helen Ross Speicher

Illustrated by Cathy Morrison

Text illustrations © 2005 Patria Press, Inc.
Cover design © 2005 Patria Press, Inc.

ISBN 1-882859-47-2 (978-1-882859-47-4) hardback
ISBN 1-882859-48-0 (978-1-882859-48-1) paperback

Patria Press, Inc.
PO Box 752
Carmel IN 46082
www.patriapress.com

Printed and bound in the United States of America

10 9 8 7 6 5 4 3 2 1

Text originally published by the Bobbs-Merrill Company, 1968, in the Childhood
of Famous Americans Series.* The Childhood of Famous Americans Series* is a
registered trademark of Simon & Schuster, Inc.

Library of Congress Cataloging-in-Publication Data

Borland, Kathryn Kilby.
  Phillis Wheatley : young Revolutionary poet / by Kathryn Kilby Borland and
Helen Ross Speicher ; illustrated by Cathy Morrison.– 2nd ed.
    p. ; cm. – (Young patriots series ; v. 10)
  ISBN-10: 1-882859-47-2
  ISBN-10: 1-882859-48-0 (pbk.)
  ISBN-13: 978-1-882859-47-4
  ISBN-13: 978-1-882859-48-1 (pbk.) 1. Wheatley, Phillis,
1753-1784–Juvenile literature. 2. Poets, American–Colonial period, ca.
1600-1775–Biography–Juvenile literature. 3. Slaves–United
States–Biography–Juvenile literature. 4. African American
poets–Biography–Juvenile literature. I. Speicher, Helen Ross. II.
Morrison, Cathy, ill. III. Title. IV. Young patriots series ; 10.

PS866.W5Z58 2005
  811'.1–dc22

2004028710

Edited by: Harold Underdown
Design by: Timothy Mayer

Contents

Illustrations

Chapter 1

Phillis Is
A Pretty Name

"What am I bid for this strong, healthy girl?" the auctioneer asked.

The crowd on the Boston wharf on this June morning in 1761 laughed. The small black girl actually looked very frail. She was wrapped in a piece of ragged carpet, but she shivered and coughed in a cool breeze.

"Surely somebody could use this good helper in the kitchen," the auctioneer coaxed.

"I'll take her," a soft voice spoke. One of two well-dressed white women standing at the edge of the crowd pushed her way forward slowly. The auctioneer took the money she held out and shoved the child toward her.

"You must be out of your mind, Susannah Wheatley," the woman's friend said. "When John told you to buy a girl to help Sukey in the kitchen, he meant a strong girl. This girl will just be a burden to Sukey."

"She looked so little and frightened that I had to take her," Mrs. Wheatley said. "You know how I feel about slavery."

"What about Sukey and Prince?"

"Sukey's been with us all her life, and she wouldn't be happy anywhere else. Prince was given to Mr. Wheatley by a man who owed him a large bill. He is working out his freedom ."

"Well," her friend responded, "it's odd that you're here in a slave market when you don't believe in slavery."

Soon they reached their carriage, where a tall black man waited. He opened the carriage door. Mrs. Wheatley motioned for the little girl to enter, but the child shrank back and started to cry softly.

"Put her in the carriage if she won't enter herself, Prince," said Mrs. Wentworth.

"Yes, Mrs. Wentworth," Prince replied, but he looked at Mrs. Wheatley.

"Just a minute, Prince," Mrs. Wheatley said. "The poor child is frightened."

Mrs. Wheatley put her hand under the little girl's chin and looked down into her watery eyes. "We are your friends, child," she said softly. "Don't be afraid."

Mrs. Wentworth sniffed. "As if she could understand a word you say!" she laughed.

"She looked so little and frightened that I had to take her," Mrs. Wheatley said. "You know how I feel about slavery."

"Of course she doesn't, but she can understand the way I say it." Mrs. Wheatley held out her hand to the child and they climbed into the carriage. The little girl sat close beside Mrs. Wheatley and closed her eyes. She was still shivering.

Mrs. Wentworth stared at the child. "How old do you think she is, Susannah?"

"I would say she is about seven. She has some front teeth missing, and that's the age when Nat and Mary lost theirs."

❖

Prince stopped to let Mrs. Wentworth out at her home. A few minutes later the carriage came to a big brick house, where the Wheatleys lived. Mrs. Wheatley and the girl got out, went up the front steps, and on through the door.

A tall girl came racing down from upstairs. She was running so fast that she had to stop herself by bumping into the wall. "Mary, are you six or sixteen?" her mother asked, smiling.

"Gracious, Mother, is that Sukey's new helper?"

"She'll grow. I had to bring her home. She looked so little and afraid."

"Yes, Mother, she's even afraid of me." Mary got down on her knees and put her arms around the little girl. "Doesn't she know we wouldn't hurt her?

What are we going to do with her? How will we teach her to talk?"

"I don't know," Mrs. Wheatley said. "You'll have to help me. The first thing is to wash her and find her some clothes. Go help Sukey fill a tub by the fire in the kitchen."

Sukey was sleeping in her chair by the fire. When she saw the girl with Mrs. Wheatley and Mary, she shook her head. "Where'd that mite come from?" she asked. "I reckon that's not the help you were going to bring me."

"Never mind about help," Mrs. Wheatley said. "Right now the girl needs a bath."

"I guess she does," Sukey sniffed. "And she needs some food and she needs her hair untangled. We need to burn that filthy old carpet she's wearing for a dress."

Sukey helped Mary fill a big wooden tub with water from a kettle hanging in the fireplace.

"I reckon I'll need help to hold her in here," Sukey said. "She'll die scared if she gets wet all over at the same time."

To their surprise, the child enjoyed being in the tub. She filled her hands with water and let it trickle out between her fingers. She made little excited noises.

"Perhaps she lived near a river and played in the water," Mary said.

When Mr. Wheatley came home that evening, Sukey had cooked his favorite dinner, baked ham and cornbread. Usually everyone saved news to tell at the table. Tonight Mrs. Wheatley asked Mr. Wheatley what had happened at his tailoring shop during the day. She asked Mary's twin, Nat, what he had done at Latin School, but she hardly listened to their answers.

Mary said nothing. Once in a while she looked at her mother, and her mother shook her head. At last the strawberries and cake were brought in. Mrs. Wheatley nodded at Mary.

Mary dashed to the kitchen and came back, leading the little girl. The child's small, thin face seemed to float over a long white petticoat which completely covered her feet and trailed on the floor. They had cut her dark hair close to her head.

"Doesn't she look nice, Father?" Mary asked proudly. "We combed her hair and found some clean clothes for her to wear."

"Goodness!" Mr. Wheatley laid down his spoon. "Is this supposed to be the new helper for old Sukey?"

Mrs. Wheatley nodded her head. She looked at him anxiously. Mr. Wheatley merely shook his head and started to laugh. The little girl broke loose from Mary's hand and ran to the kitchen.

Then Mrs. Wheatley explained what had happened

in the market that morning. "Well, I might have known you'd bring me home a helpless creature," Mr. Wheatley said. But he said it as if he were proud of her.

Mary went to the kitchen and soon came back with the child so close behind her that Mr. Wheatley could see only the ruffle of the white petticoat. Finally Mary coaxed her to come and sit on her lap. She sat there stiffly, her bright eyes wide open.

"Her bones almost show through her skin," Mr. Wheatley said. "Has she had anything to eat?"

"Sukey tried to feed her, but she wouldn't eat anything," Mary said.

"Wouldn't eat? The child's starving. Of course she'll eat." He held out a strawberry. The child looked at it but did not reach for it.

"Try this." Nat gave up half a slice of his pound cake. Mary held it to the child's mouth, but she turned her head away.

"She's certainly not used to our food," Mary said. "If only we knew what she used to eat."

Mrs. Wheatley smiled. "You may be right, but she'll soon learn to like baked beans and codfish cakes instead. Now she needs a good night's sleep."

"Can't we name her first, Mother?" Mary asked. "Let's give her a pretty name."

"How's Aphrodite?" Nat asked. "Or maybe Penelope?"

"Don't be silly, Nat," Mary said. "She's too little for a long name."

"Phillis is a pretty name," Mrs. Wheatley suggested thoughtfully.

"Phillis," Mary repeated softly. "Phillis. I like that name." The child looked up at Mary and, for the first time, smiled.

"She likes it, too," Mr. Wheatley said. "Her name will be Phillis."

Chapter 2

So Much to Learn

Mary opened her eyes. It was light, but the sun wasn't shining yet. She hardly ever woke up so early. Suddenly she heard a loud crash of breaking china.

She sat up in bed so that she could check on Phillis. But the little mattress Phillis slept on at the foot of Mary's bed was empty.

Mary ran into the hall. Her father and Nat were already there. Her mother was running downstairs. Phillis was sitting at the foot of the stairs, crying. Mary's water pitcher, with its pink painted roses, was broken into a hundred pieces.

Phillis jumped up and ran to an east window. She pointed excitedly out the window and spoke in her own language. Then she hurried back to the stairs and frantically tried to scoop up some of the water on the floor.

"Evidently she wants water," said Nat, leaning over the banister.

"Mary, take her out to the kitchen and get her a glass of water," said Mr. Wheatley. "Then we can go back to bed."

"I don't think she's thirsty, Father."

"Then why does she want water?" asked Mrs. Wheatley thoughtfully.

Phillis pointed out the window and began to cry again. Mary went over to the window beside her. "There's nothing to cry about out there, Phillis," she said. "The sun is up, and it's going to be a beautiful day."

Later that morning Mary brought Phillis down to the kitchen, and Sukey gave her a piece of bread to eat before breakfast. At first Phillis looked at the bread suspiciously, but finally she took a tiny bite. Then she held it tightly in both hands and ate it quickly. When she finished, she held out her hand to Sukey, and Sukey gave her another piece.

As Phillis held out her hand for the fourth time, Mrs. Wheatley came into the kitchen. "Since she's hungry, perhaps she'll try something else," she suggested.

Sukey put some oatmeal into a bowl and set it on the table in front of Phillis. The child looked at it and turned away.

The next few days were rainy, and Mary and Phillis stayed in the house. At first Phillis stayed close to

Mary. Then gradually she began to trust others, too. Her appetite grew along with her trust in the family. Not only did she eat the foods that Mary coaxed her to try, but she tried soap and silver polish.

"There's nothing in the house she doesn't want to taste," Sukey remarked. But she smiled as she watched Phillis scampering around.

The next sunny morning, Mary woke up with the feeling that something was wrong. She sat up and looked at Phillis' bed. It was empty.

Mary ran out into the hall. There was no sign of Phillis. Then she heard a small sound from the kitchen and ran quietly downstairs. There she found Phillis pounding on the heavy locked door. Beside her on the floor was a big white pitcher.

When Phillis saw Mary she pointed to the window and began to cry. Once again Mary saw only a beautiful sunrise. When she told the others at breakfast, none of them could guess what Phillis wanted.

"It's something outdoors," Nat said.

"And she needs water for it," Mary said.

"And she wants the water in a pitcher for some reason," Mr. Wheatley added. "It may be some kind of ritual."

"Mary," Nat said, "Let's leave the kitchen door unlocked tonight. Then when she gets up, we can follow her and see what she does."

"Do you approve, Mother?" Mary asked.

"Well, if we can find out what she wants to do, perhaps we can help," Mrs. Wheatley said, "provided your father agrees to leaving the door unlocked."

"There won't be much danger in leaving the door unlocked," Mr. Wheatley said, "and I want to stop this nonsense. I can't afford to go on buying pitchers forever."

Mary promised to knock on Nat's wall as soon as Phillis left their room in the morning. But in the morning Mary found rain spitting against her window. Phillis slept peacefully until Mary got up.

"She needs sunshine for the ritual," Nat said. "When it stops raining, we'll try again."

The next morning the sky began to lighten very early. Mary woke up and lay with her eyes closed.

At last she heard Phillis stirring about. Then she heard a rustling of the covers. Careful not to seem to be awake, Mary peered out through her eyelashes. Phillis dressed very quickly and tiptoed over to Mary's little mahogany bureau.

Carefully she lifted the heavy pitcher of water and crept to the door. She set the pitcher down gently while she opened the door. Then she slipped through and closed it without making a sound.

As soon as Phillis closed the door, Mary quickly dressed. When she was sure Phillis was downstairs, she knocked softly on Nat's wall. By the time she reached the head of the stairs, he was out of his room. Quickly the two of them hurried downstairs into the kitchen. They found the back door open, but no sign of Phillis. Quietly they stepped out into the cool early morning air. There they found Phillis facing the sun which was just coming up, red and beautiful.

She poured water out of the pitcher onto the ground. She bent over and touched her forehead to the ground. Then she stood up and held her thin arms out toward the sun. On her face was a radiant smile.

❖

"She's worshipping the sun, as she did at home," Nat said softly.

When Phillis heard them she took several steps backward and looked as if she might cry. Mary and Nat hadn't noticed that their mother was standing behind them. She said, "Phillis, there's nothing to be afraid of. Nobody's going to be angry with you."

Phillis picked up the pitcher and ran to Mrs. Wheatley. She pointed to Mary and then she pointed to Mrs. Wheatley. She made motions of pouring.

"I have no idea what she's trying to tell us," Mrs. Wheatley said.

"I know!" Mary said excitedly. "She's telling us that her mother did what she's doing."

Then she stood up and held her thin arms out toward
the sun. On her face was a radiant smile.

"You're right, Mary!" Nat said. "Her mother worshipped the sun god by pouring out water just as the sun came up in the morning. That's why she couldn't do it on a rainy day."

At the breakfast table Mary and Nat told their father what Phillis had done. Mr. Wheatley listened while he buttered a piece of warm bread.

"Let's hope that she'll now be content to stay in bed in the morning until the rest of us get up," he said.

Mrs. Wheatley shook her head. "No, I doubt that she will," she said.

"Well, we can't have her getting up early every morning when the sun shines," said Mr. Wheatley.

"But it's her religion," said Mrs. Wheatley. "It's her way of worshipping God, the only way she knows. It's the way she learned in Africa before she came here."

"Then do we let her go on tramping around and breaking pitchers?" Mr. Wheatley asked.

"I know what we can do," said Mrs. Wheatley. "We'll give her a little pitcher to use in place of the big one. Letting her do something familiar will comfort her."

"You are right as usual, my dear," Mr. Wheatley commented.

Phillis' eyes glowed when Mrs. Wheatley handed her a small blue and white cream pitcher that night when she was ready for bed. Mary helped her fill it with water, and she set it on the floor beside her mattress.

In a few days the family became used to the sound of Phillis' tiptoeing downstairs every sunny morning.

By now Phillis ate heartily with the members of the family and no longer tasted things around the house. She looked far different from the little girl Mrs. Wheatley had found on the Boston wharf. But she still was thin and coughed a great deal, which worried Mrs. Wheatley.

"The child still is delicate," Mrs. Wheatley said to Sukey. "She needs good food and plenty of rest and sunshine every day."

"If it's food she needs it won't take long to do the job," Sukey said. "That girl must be hollow all the way through."

One day when Mary woke after the sun had risen, she found Phillis asleep. The little blue and white pitcher still stood on the floor beside her, half full of water. After that, Phillis crept downstairs a few more times. Then one morning she put the small pitcher beside Mary's big one on the bureau and left it there.

Mrs. Wheatley and Mary made dresses for Phillis. They were plain, dark cotton dresses, with little white scarves tied in front. She wore ruffled white caps with them, as most New England girls did.

Phillis was proud of her new clothes. She loved to stand in front of the long mirror in Mary's room, making faces at herself and giggling. However, Phillis did not see any good reason to wear the long hot dresses on warm summer days. One day Mary looked out the back door and saw Phillis' long gray dress draped over a rosebush. Her stiff petticoat covered another bush. Phillis sat under a chestnut tree in her long underdrawers, fanning herself with a big leaf.

That afternoon Mrs. Wheatley found her sitting on the front porch wearing only her petticoat. She shooed her into the house, hoping none of the neighbors had seen.

"There's just no way to make her understand," she sighed.

"She understands what she wants to understand," Sukey grumbled. "It's time that girl learned to talk. She'll learn fast, whenever she makes up her mind."

Chapter 3

Say "Apple"

"Ap-ple, Phillis. Say ap-ple," Mary repeated patiently. But Phillis wasn't looking at the apple. She was watching a red bird on a bush beside the open kitchen door.

Nat stopped in the doorway. "You don't seem to be making much progress," he said. "Phillis is smart, but I'm beginning to wonder if she'll ever learn to speak English."

"Of course she will," Mary said. "I can tell by the look in her eyes. It will just take patience and love."

"Look, Phillis. Apple. Eat." Mary took a bite out of the apple and held it out toward Phillis.

The girl looked at it curiously, but did not touch it.

"Mary," Mrs. Wheatley called from upstairs. Mary dashed out of the room. When she came back later, Phillis had disappeared. Every apple in the bowl had one big bite taken out.

While Mary was still looking at the apples, Sukey

called from the pantry. "Now look what that Phillis did. She ate half the cake I saved for supper. Miss Susannah said to give her all she wanted to eat, but there's no filling her up. Where has she gone?"

"I don't know," Mary answered. "She just disappeared a few minutes ago."

"She's probably around somewhere looking for something to eat," Sukey said, smiling. "Things surely will be easier around here when she learns to speak English."

❖

Just then a large onion came rolling out from under the kitchen table, followed by Phillis on all fours. She was shedding big drops of tears and clawing frantically at her mouth. "Well, it looks like she finally has tried one thing too many," Sukey laughed.

"Here, Phillis." Mary handed her a cup of water, but Phillis shook her head. "Apple," she said plainly in a high clear voice.

"Sukey," Mary called, "did you hear?"

Sukey took her head out of the big brick oven. "Hear what, Miss Mary?"

"Did you hear Phillis speak? She said 'apple.' Say it again, Phillis." But Phillis merely grabbed the apple Mary held out to her and ran out the door into the sunshine.

"I reckon you wanted her to talk so bad that you imagined she did."

"No, Sukey. She really did speak, but you had your head in the oven."

"If your mother had brought home a helper that didn't eat faster than I can cook, I wouldn't have my head in the oven most of the time," Sukey teased.

Phillis came back into the house, holding the apple core. She ran over to Mary, her eyes dancing. "Apple," she said plainly.

"She sure enough did say 'apple', even if she never says another word." Sukey threw her arms around Phillis, and Mary ran to get Nat, who came running excitedly. Then once more Mary picked up an apple.

"Apple," Phillis said excitedly.

"If she can say one thing, she can say something else," Mary said. She patted the table where Sukey was rolling out pie crust. "Table, Phillis," she said clearly.

"Table, Phillis," Phillis answered.

"She can talk! She can talk, Nat!" Mary whirled through the kitchen from fireplace to chair to window. Phillis whirled after her, laughing and repeating each word.

Finally Sukey called, "It's time to let her rest for a while, Miss Mary. You'll have her little brain all scrambled."

"She's right," Nat said. "Let her rest."

That night at dinner Mary and Nat could hardly wait to show their mother and father what Phillis could do. But Phillis wouldn't open her mouth, and Mr. Wheatley pretended he didn't believe she could say a word.

However, everyone soon had to admit that Phillis could talk. In fact, she talked and talked and talked. She followed Mary and Mrs. Wheatley everywhere, tugging at their skirts and pointing at everything in the house. In a few more weeks she was putting words together and making short sentences.

❖

One hot July afternoon Mrs. Wheatley and Mrs. Wentworth sat sipping lemonade in the cool, dark parlor. Phillis ran into the room. She ran up to Mrs. Wheatley, holding out a lemon.

"What is it? What is it?" she asked.

"It's a lemon, dear."

Mrs. Wentworth stared at her friend. "I'm surprised, Susannah, at the way you treat this child. She had no right to come and interrupt us."

"She is a small girl just learning to talk," Mrs. Wheatley explained. "We've encouraged her to ask questions."

"You're making a big mistake. Surely the other

servants can teach her anything she needs to know. At least they could teach her not to interrupt important conversations."

Mrs. Wheatley smiled sweetly. "Will you have another glass of lemonade?" she asked.

Before Mrs. Wentworth could answer, Phillis was back again. Her small face was puckered up. "Lemon bad," she said. Mrs. Wheatley laughed and hugged Phillis.

"Well, Susannah," Mrs. Wentworth said, "I can't understand what you're trying to do with this child."

"I'm sorry, Isabel. We've been enjoying teaching her so much that I forgot everyone might not feel the same way."

"You're quite right. Everyone does not." Mrs. Wentworth arose and sailed out the door.

Sukey came in for the lemonade glasses. "Here, Phillis," she said. "Please carry out this plate of cookies for me."

Phillis ran over and eagerly snatched up the plate. Then she let the plate tilt to one side and left a trail of broken sugar cookies all the way across the red-patterned rug.

Mrs. Wheatley watched as Sukey shook her head and went to get the broom and dustpan. This was one of the first times she had asked Phillis to help, and the child had only caused extra work.

Mrs. Wheatley worried about Sukey working too much, but it was fall before an answer to that problem presented itself. The answer was Sophie, owned by one of the Wheatleys' relatives, who came to stay with them when her mistress went to live in England.

Sukey did not want her to help in the kitchen, and so Sophie began training Phillis. "Here," she said one afternoon. "Fold this napkin. You fold it this way and this way and that way. It's easy."

Phillis tried to make her fingers do what Sophie's had done. But when she finished folding the napkin, it looked as if it had been used as a towel for several days.

Sophie snatched up the napkin. "Now I have to iron it again." Then, looking at Phillis' small sad face, she said more kindly, "Here, take this spoon and bag of salt and fill the little salt dishes on the table." Phillis obeyed, but she had trouble dipping salt with the large spoon and putting it in the small dishes. Soon she had more salt on the floor than in the dishes.

"If there's anything I hate, it's trying to sweep up salt," Sophie grumbled. "There must be something you can do right."

Sophie was busy setting the enormous dinner table for company. "Bring me the blue and white plates from the pantry, but bring them one at a time."

Phillis made trip after trip to the pantry. The tip of

her tongue showed at the corner of her mouth as she concentrated on each step.

At last she had carried each plate and cup and saucer to the table. Sophie was too busy to notice. Phillis reached up to tug at Sophie's sleeve. "I did it!" she said proudly. "I did it right!"

As Phillis pointed to the pile of dishes on the table her elbow brushed against a cup near the edge. Horrified, she and Sophie watched it roll to the floor, where it broke neatly in two.

"It's the best company china," Sophie groaned, picking up the two pieces. "Mrs. Wheatley will whip you for sure."

"No she wouldn't."

"Well, she won't like this," said Sophie. "You don't know what she'll do. After all, you've never broken any of her company china before. From now on maybe you should just polish silver."

All afternoon Phillis sat in the pantry polishing silver. There were big forks and little forks and medium-sized forks and five different kinds of spoons. Phillis didn't see how the guests could use so much silver, even if they used a different piece for every bite.

Every time the door opened she shivered. Each time she was sure it would be Mrs. Wheatley, coming to whip her. When Mrs. Wheatley finally came into the kitchen, Phillis dropped the fork she was polishing.

All afternoon Phillis sat in the pantry polishing silver.

"I didn't mean to," she sobbed. "I'll never do it again. Please don't be angry."

When Mrs. Wheatley heard what had happened, she went to find Sophie. Phillis didn't hear what she said, but when Sophie came back to the kitchen she was angry.

"Tattletale!" she hissed. "You'll be sorry."

Chapter 4

Everyday Living

"Where's that child who's supposed to be helping old Sukey?"

It sounded like Sukey, but the speaker was slim, eight-year-old Phillis. After a few months with the Wheatleys, Phillis was no longer timid and hungry. She was beginning to grow taller. She was learning English as fast as the family could teach her. More than that, she was becoming a first-rate mimic.

Her mischievous eyes twinkled happily as she saw Sophie look sharply around the room for Sukey. Then Sophie began polishing silver as if her life depended on it.

"You, Sophie, how come you're so slow this morning?" Phillis went on in Sukey's voice. She knew Sophie hated to polish silver and did this work only when Sukey was nearby.

Soon Sophie spied Phillis behind the pantry door. Her black eyes blazed. "How come little Miss Tattletale isn't working at cleaning something? There's plenty of cleaning in this big house. How come I don't see you working?"

Phillis laughed gaily. She held out a feather duster almost as big as she was. "I am," she replied. "I'm dusting furniture."

Sophie snorted. "In the pantry? Maybe you can fool some folks, but not me."

"I'm deli-cate," Phillis said. This time she mimicked Mrs. Wheatley's voice. "I'm not supposed to do any hard work."

"You certainly don't," Sophie said.

"Mrs. Wheatley says I'm fas-cin-a-ting," Phillis laughed with Mrs. Wheatley's voice.

"Sukey doesn't think you're fascinating," came a third voice. "You act too smarty and nobody likes it. Get along now. You're supposed to be dusting."

"That Phillis hardly does anything for her keep," Sophie complained to Sukey.

"She still is not very strong."

"The best way to make her strong is to put her in the kitchen, where she was supposed to work from the start," Sophie retorted.

"But she wasn't supposed to work in the kitchen," explained Sukey. "She was too weak and frail when she came here to do any kind of work. Now she is stronger, but still not strong enough to work in the kitchen."

Phillis quietly listened to this conversation and smiled.

Then Prince walked into the room and Phillis went to stand behind Prince and Sukey. She began to imitate them, one after the other. First she pretended to be the stiff, tall coachman. Then she imitated the bent-over figure of Sukey and pretended to set the table. Both Prince and Sukey greatly enjoyed the mimicking activities, and Phillis knew they were pleased.

Suddenly Sophie spoke up. "Stop having fun. Just because Mrs. Wheatley didn't punish you for breaking that cup the other day was no sign she was happy about it. Would you like to have her sell you to a man like the one who had you first?"

"Oh, no!" Phillis was horrified.

"That what happens to girls who don't work hard and mind their manners," Sophie said, hoping to frighten Phillis.

"I'll try, Sophie. I don't ever want to see that man again." Phillis broke into sobs and began to tremble. For a while after this she was as obedient as she could be.

After breakfast one Sunday morning in the fall Mrs. Wheatley said, "Phillis, you are to go to church with us today."

"Sometimes the sermon lasts two hours," Mary

said doubtfully. "Do you think you can be quiet that long, Phillis?"

"If you want me to, I can," Phillis promised, her dark eyes solemn.

"Good. Then put on your new dark blue dress," Mrs. Wheatley ordered gently.

"Oh, thank you. I like that blue dress. It's my favorite," Phillis said. She had several plain dresses for everyday, but her new blue dress had a lovely lace-edged collar. This would be the first time she had worn it.

"Have Prince bring the carriage around in an hour, Nat," Mrs. Wheatley said.

Phillis was excited. "I'm going to church with you this morning," she announced happily to Sophie. She now shared Sophie's room.

"Are you really?" Sophie looked at her curiously. She might have stared the same way at a mouse that came out of his hole to dance a jig in the middle of the room.

"Yes, and I'm to wear my new dress, too." Phillis smiled happily.

"Of course you'll sit in the gallery with Sukey and me," said Sophie, "and all the while you must be very quiet."

"I know. Will Prince sit with us?"

"Yes, but he won't sit by you. I'm going to sit by

you, and you'd better be quiet. Not one wiggle, not one yawn, not one sneeze out of you the whole time!"

"I'll be quiet. You'll see."

"You better be. Folks sometimes sell slaves who can't sit still in church."

"Mr. Wheatley wouldn't."

"You can't tell," Sophie said, glancing slyly at her. "He might, since you don't do much work around here anyhow."

Phillis started to dress and tried to forget what Sophie had said. She made sure her unruly curls were almost hidden under her little ruffled cap. She tucked a clean white handkerchief into her pocket. She gave her black leather shoes an extra rubbing. It didn't matter which shoe she put on which foot because both shoes were made exactly alike.

Sophie asked Phillis to button the tiny buttons down the back of her dress. Phillis tried, but her fingers shook so that Sophie had to finish buttoning the dress herself.

When Phillis was ready she began to tremble so that she could hardly walk down the stairs. "Do you feel all right?" Mrs. Wheatley asked her as she and the other Wheatley servants gathered for a final inspection in front of the carriage block at the front door.

"Yes, ma'am, I'm all right," Phillis answered, but her teeth were chattering. Mr. and Mrs. Wheatley

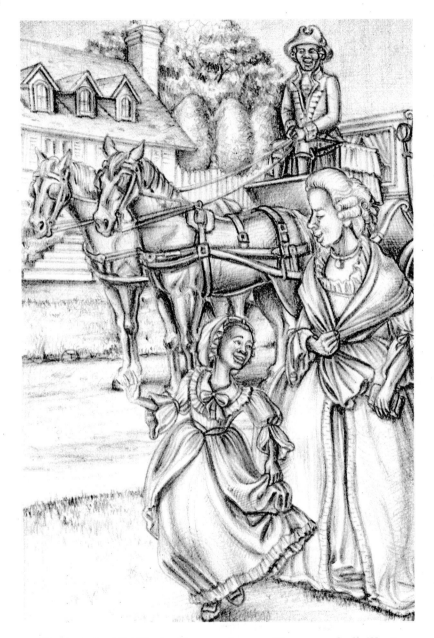

"Let's take Phillis in the carriage with us, and she'll sit with us instead of with the servants during the service."

exchanged glances.

"Do you suppose she has the ague?" Mr. Wheatley asked anxiously.

"I shouldn't think so," his wife replied thoughtfully, "but perhaps we should take her with us in the carriage."

"That's an excellent suggestion. The wind is downright chilly this morning."

Sukey spoke up. "Phillis is shaking because she is afraid."

"Afraid? Why should she be afraid?" Mr. Wheatley asked.

"She's afraid you will sell her."

"Impossible!" Mr. Wheatley was shocked. "Who has given her any such idea as that?"

"Sophie." Sukey ignored Sophie's glare. "I heard them talking this morning while they dressed." Mr. Wheatley's face turned pale with anger. Sophie took a step backward.

"Sophie, how could you?" Mrs. Wheatley was almost as furious as her husband.

Mr. Wheatley added, "I'll talk to you later, Sophie, but I don't wish to be late for church. Let's take Phillis in the carriage with us, and she'll sit with us instead of with the servants during the service."

"Come and sit between Nat and me," Mary called from the carriage. "But don't muss my new taffeta dress. It just came with Papa's latest shipment from England."

"I won't muss it," Phillis promised as she snuggled down between the twins. Nat was dressed like his father in a sober black suit with a ruffled white linen shirtfront.

Prince cracked his whip over the backs of the bays, and away they pranced down King Street. Phillis leaned back and smiled. She'd never believe Sophie again in her life.

Chapter 5

It's Too Cold

"**M**ary, get your ice skates and I'll take you and Phillis to the Commons. The Frog Pond is frozen over, and everybody's there." Nat's face was cherry red from the cold. He stamped his feet and held his numbed fingers in front of the parlor fireplace.

"Oh, good!" Mary cried, running up the stairs. "Get your warm cape, Phillis."

"Have they lighted the bonfires around the pond?" asked Mrs. Wheatley. "Those bonfires always look so cheerful." She smiled as she thought of the fun the children would have skating. Mr. Wheatley laid his book aside and rose from his comfortable chair to place another birch log on the blazing fire. This winter of 1764 was very cold.

"Yes, there are almost a dozen fires," Nat explained, "but more skaters keep coming all the time. The place is so crowded that it is hard to get close to the fires."

Mary came back into the room with her warm

cloak on, and started to tuck her hair under her hood. "Come on," Nat urged. "Frog Pond will thaw out and the children will be sailing toy boats on it before you get your hair fixed."

"You never can tell who'll be out skating," Mary said, flashing a smile and dealing with one last stray curl. "Well, I'm ready. Let's go." She flung her skates over her shoulder and turned to the door.

"How about Phillis?" Nat asked.

"Mr. Nat, I'm sorry, it's too cold for me," said Phillis.

"Come on, Phillis," Nat said. "You won't mind the cold after you get used to it."

"No, thank you, Mr. Nat," Phillis answered. "If I go out, I'll be cold all night long. When the wind whistles the way it does tonight, my feet feel like two blocks of ice. I'd rather sit by the fire and read the Bible for a while, if I may."

"Of course you may, Phillis, if you're sure you don't want to go," said Mrs. Wheatley.

Phillis shivered and hurried over to the fireplace. She bowed her small curly head over the big family Bible.

"We're off," the twins called. As they opened the heavy front door, a stream of cold air crept across the floor. Their parents shivered, and Mr. Wheatley carefully added another log to the fire.

Phillis was soon deep in her favorite story of the ninety-and-nine sheep safe in the fold. She loved to reread the part about the good shepherd going out to look for the little lamb. She had read all the way

Phillis was soon deep in her favorite story of the ninety-and-nine sheep safe in the fold.

through the Bible twice, and she had read every other book the Wheatleys owned. She had read books on astronomy, histories of both the modern and ancient worlds, and stories of gods and goddesses.

Mrs. Wheatley sighed. "I'm sorry that Phillis didn't feel like going skating with Nat and Mary," she said to Mr. Wheatley.

"We must give her time to gain strength," Mr. Wheatley said.

Mrs. Wheatley's face brightened. "Yes, but did you ever see a ten-year-old child take such an interest in reading?"

"I had hoped to have some new books for us to read by now," said Mr. Wheatley. "But the new Navigation Acts have interfered with my usual shipments from England."

"I think the Sugar Act is worse," Mrs. Wheatley replied. "You'll have to forget about baked beans for dinner. I will not buy molasses for them so long as England insists on such an unfair tax."

"Maybe we should send you to England to plead our cause," Mr. Wheatley teased gently.

"I'm not the only one who's upset," Mrs. Wheatley retorted. "All my friends are refusing to buy molasses so long as it is taxed."

"A three-penny tax isn't so much."

"Nat says it's not just the tax, but the fact that it may be only a beginning."

"Come now, my dear. Don't begin quoting a college boy. He is exaggerating a small inconvenience."

"You are hard to understand, Mr. Wheatley. You send Nat to Harvard to learn to use his mind. Then you refuse to listen to him when he has an idea different from yours."

"Sometimes his ideas are wild. Britain is keeping soldiers here to protect us from the Indians. Nat argues that Britain—our own country—may turn the soldiers against us—her own colonies. That's absurd."

"Well, let's not talk any more about it now," Mrs. Wheatley said. "I'm as chilly as Phillis. It's time for us to go to bed."

❖

Phillis rose from her reading reluctantly. She disliked leaving the warm fire for the cold bedroom. Even though she slept between the scratchy folds of a wool blanket, she never felt really warm in such cold weather.

"Good-night, Mrs. Wheatley. Good-night, Mr. Wheatley," she murmured obediently.

She was shivering as she started for the back stairs, and by morning she was shaking so hard that the bed rocked. All night she had turned and tossed. Sophie complained that she hadn't had a wink of sleep all night.

Mrs. Wheatley came into their room to see what

was wrong. "Do you hurt somewhere, Phillis?" she asked softly.

Phillis lay back on her pillow, too tired to answer. Only her eyes seemed alive. "I just don't feel good any place," she whispered.

Mrs. Wheatley immediately pulled Sophie out into the hall and sent her to tell Prince to go for Dr. Warren. "Tell Prince to hurry," she said. "When Phillis was ill last fall, the doctor said he would be afraid for her life if she became ill again this winter. Now go!"

Mrs. Wheatley hurried back to the room to put another blanket over Phillis, who now lay very still under the patchwork quilt.

Chapter 6

Latin and Tension

"Now, try again, Phillis," Mary said. "What's
the word for carry?"

"*Ferio*. No, that means cut. *Fero* means carry. I
always get those mixed up."

Phillis was sitting up in bed with her throat
wrapped in red flannel. Mary sat beside her in a
straight chair. They were so interested that they
didn't hear Mrs. Wheatley greeting guests in the hall
downstairs. Suddenly Evelyn Wentworth stood in the
door of Phillis' bedroom, shaking raindrops from her
gray fur muff.

"What are you doing?" she asked. "And what's
Phillis doing in this room?"

"Mother put Phillis here so we can take care of
her better. She has been very ill. Dr. Warren has been
here several times. Now we're learning Latin."

"You're what?" Evelyn cried.

"We're learning Latin," Mary replied. "Nat teaches

me, and then I teach Phillis."

Evelyn began to laugh. "Then she can teach Sukey and Sophie, and they can talk Latin while they peel potatoes."

Phillis felt her face getting hot. Evelyn Wentworth always made her feel as if she wasn't supposed to learn anything.

"All of you wait on Phillis as if she were a princess instead of a servant girl," Evelyn went on. She looked around the neat room with its blue braided rug and white curtains.

Mary stood up. Her face was red. "We don't think of Phillis either as a princess or a servant girl. Shall we go downstairs?" She straightened Phillis's covers and patted her shoulder before she left.

Phillis couldn't help overhearing the conversation when the older girls joined their mothers in the parlor. "You'd never guess what they're doing with Phillis now," Evelyn told her mother. "Mary's teaching her Latin."

"Latin?" Mrs. Wentworth's voice was scornful. "How can Mary teach her Latin?"

"Nat's been helping them with it," Mrs. Wheatley said proudly.

"Susannah, don't you know it is dangerous for females to study too hard? Reading, arithmetic, embroidery, and a little music and dancing are all a girl needs to know. Anything more will tax her brain. I would never think of taxing Evelyn's brain."

Phillis smiled. She was sure anyone could see that Evelyn's brain had not been taxed.

"They've even given her the room next to Mary's," Evelyn went on indignantly.

"Evelyn, you must not criticize the household arrangements of others, no matter how strange they are," Mrs. Wentworth said coldly.

"I'm happy to hear you say that, Isabel," Mrs. Wheatley said crisply. "Otherwise I would think you are a busybody, and I am sure you are not."

Phillis could imagine how Mrs. Wheatley looked when she said this. She would be smiling politely, but the look in her eyes would make Mrs. Wentworth ashamed of herself.

The front door opened noisily and Nat stormed in. He dropped his books with a thud on the table in the hall. Usually he rushed to the kitchen to see what Sukey had to eat, but today he hurried into the parlor.

"Something will happen tomorrow," Phillis heard him say excitedly. "Men are standing around talking everywhere. And they're angrier than I've ever heard them before."

"Why should anything happen tomorrow?" Mrs. Wentworth asked.

"Because tomorrow's the first of November, and that's the day the Stamp Act goes into effect," Nat answered.

"They talk, but they won't defy the king," Mrs. Wentworth said.

Nat didn't answer Mrs. Wentworth. Pretty soon Phillis heard him go out to the kitchen. She liked to hear him talk about people being angry with the king about taxes. Yet it frightened her—she was afraid he would get into trouble.

Frowning, Phillis picked up her favorite book about the ancient Greek and Roman gods and goddesses. She liked the stories, but even more she loved the beautiful words that sounded so important and poetical. She repeated a few of the words out loud to herself as she read. "The palaces of the illustrious gods." "To the stars she addressed her incantations." "The magic contents of the cauldron."

Phillis soon found herself trying to think of words to rhyme with the beautiful words in the story. What words, she wondered, would rhyme with *incantation*? She thought of *education, declaration, fascination*. She came to the word *illustrious*. What would rhyme with this? At first she couldn't think of any, but she remembered *industrious*.

That night after supper Mary brought Nat to Phillis's room so he could hear what she had learned that day. "It's a good thing you have to depend on me to bring the lessons home," he said, after he had listened to her recitation. "Otherwise you'd be way ahead of me."

"Mr. Nat," Phillis asked, "do you really think something bad will happen tomorrow?"

"That depends upon what you call bad," Nat answered thoughtfully. "I don't think people will pay the Stamp Tax."

"Why won't they?"

"Because the more taxes they pay without having anything to say about them, the more taxes there'll be," Nat explained.

"Are the taxes big?" Phillis asked.

"Big enough to make people angry," Nat said. "Besides they cause people all kinds of bother. Every legal paper must be printed on special paper or brought to a stamp office to be stamped. Every copy of a newspaper must have a stamp which costs a shilling. Every copy of an almanac must have a stamp which costs four shillings. But worse than all that is the fact that England would think we can be taxed without our consent."

That night Phillis could hardly sleep. She kept wondering what the colonists would do the next day. She hoped they would not defy the king. It would be too dangerous.

The next morning she felt much better, but Mrs. Wheatley thought she should stay in bed one more day. She had hoped to hear Mr. Wheatley and Nat talk at breakfast. She knew Mr. Wheatley thought Nat was wrong in believing the people would defy the king.

She and Mary started working on their Latin after breakfast, but neither of them was really thinking about it. Phillis knew she was making many mistakes, but Mary didn't notice.

"Do you hear bells, Miss Mary?" Phillis asked. "I've thought I heard bells all morning."

"I haven't noticed, Phillis." Mary went to the window and opened it. Now they could hear the bells plainly.

"Listen! There are guns being fired, too." Phillis shivered.

Mr. Wheatley came home long before noon. "Boston is like a dead city," he said. "Nearly every business is closed. Bells are being rung and flags are at half staff, as if a funeral procession were going by. Guns are being fired. I heard that the bells were being rung one-hundred-and-forty-five times to show that liberty died in America at the age of one hundred and forty-five, but I didn't count."

"Has there been any of the violence that Nat expected?" Mrs. Wheatley asked.

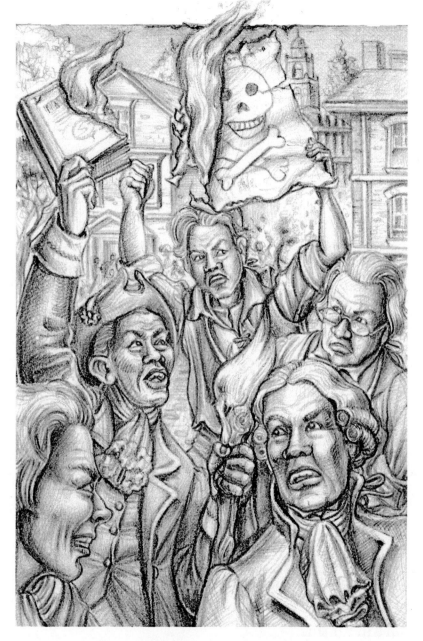

"It's unthinkable," Mr. Wheatley said.
"Boston has gone absolutely mad. . . ."

"Not so far. But the day isn't over, and there's danger in the air."

He went out again after dinner. When he came home late that afternoon, he called, "Nat! Nat!" before he had even taken off his coat. Mary ran downstairs. Phillis ran to the top of the stairway where she could hear.

"I hope Nat isn't mixed up in this," Mr. Wheatley said. "I didn't think they'd do it."

"Do what, Father? What did they do?"

"It's unthinkable," Mr. Wheatley said. "Boston has gone absolutely mad. A howling mob pulled down the stamp collector's little shop. Then they swarmed into the homes of the royal customs collectors and Chief Justice Hutchinson. They even burned furniture and tossed books into the street."

"Oh, no," Mary gasped. "What can they possibly do next?"

❖

The hall door opened and Nat ran in. "I told you something would happen," he said excitedly. "Wasn't it splendid?"

"Do you call arson and destruction and lawlessness splendid?" asked his father. "I hope you had no part in all this."

"No, Father," replied Nat. "I wouldn't have minded

helping destroy the stamped paper, but I could never have burned furniture and books. The mob went too far, but it was splendid that they defied the king. They showed him we'll never pay the tax."

"Mobs always go too far," Mr. Wheatley said. "This may make the king more determined than ever to show his power. There are lawful ways to persuade him to remove an unfair tax."

"What other ways are there?" Nat cried. "He's been begged and petitioned and pleaded with, but all he does is invent new taxes for us to pay. He'll never take the taxes off unless we resist and resist and resist."

"Enough, Nat," roared his father. "I'll hear no more of this kind of talk. Boston must not be ruled by a mob."

Phillis suddenly felt cold and weak. She hurried back to bed and pulled the covers up to her chin. She had a feeling that she could see terrible trouble ahead. She wished King George would take off this tax so things could be the way they were before.

Chapter 7

A Poem to King George

P hillis sat up in bed. It wasn't daylight. Some sound must have awakened her, but now the night was quiet. She lay back and closed her eyes, wondering whether she was mistaken. Then she heard a bell ringing, again and again, louder and louder.

She ran to open her window and leaned out into the warm May darkness. A man on horseback came galloping down the street. He was shouting, but Phillis could not understand what he said.

Now she could hear Mr. Wheatley's window being thrown up with an angry sound. "What's all this?" he called out angrily.

"Good news! Good news!" the horseman shouted, but he didn't slow down.

Phillis saw lighted windows in other houses up and down the street. One or two men had come out on the front steps with dressing gowns over their nightshirts.

"What is it?" they called to one another, but nobody seemed to know.

Before long a group of young men came running down the street with lighted torches. They were throwing their hats in the air.

"Three cheers for King George! Three cheers for the Sons of Liberty!" they shouted. Mr. Wheatley got the attention of one of the young men.

"We have good news about the Stamp Act, sir," the man called. "Word just came that the Stamp Act has been repealed!"

Phillis could hear Nat's shout from his room. "We did it! We did it!"

No one in the Wheatley household, or probably in all of Boston, went back to sleep that night. The bells went on ringing. Soon drums were beating steadily, and once in a while the boom of a cannon could be heard.

Breakfast next morning was a happy meal. Everyone was hungry after the excitement of the night. Sukey beamed as she brought in huge platters of codfish cakes and corn bread.

"Well," Mrs. Wheatley said, "from now on Boston should be the way it used to be. No more riots. No more Sons of Liberty."

"Oh, I think we'll still have Sons of Liberty, Mother," Nat said. "We want to be sure England doesn't try anything else."

"Don't speak of England as if it were a foreign country, Nat," his father said. "We shall always be English."

"Of course we will, Father, no matter where we live. But we want to be treated like all other Englishmen."

The clock in the hall struck eight, and still Mr. Wheatley sat at the table with his family. "Aren't you going to the shop today, John?" Mrs. Wheatley asked.

"Not today," Mr. Wheatley replied. "This will be a holiday in all of Boston."

"Can Nat take Phillis and me out to see the excitement?" Mary asked.

"Certainly he can, unless he has other plans," Mr. Wheatley answered.

"No, not really," Nat answered slowly. Phillis was sure Nat would rather have gone by himself.

By the time Mary and Phillis were ready, crowds of people were filling the narrow streets. Most of them were dressed in their best Sunday clothes. Flags were waving from many of the houses, and everybody was laughing.

As Nat, Mary, and Phillis turned toward the Commons, Phillis said, "Oh, look at the Liberty Tree. Isn't it exciting?" The enormous elm tree had been named the Liberty Tree because it was one of the favorite meeting places of the Sons of Liberty. Now flags and colored streamers of every color hung from its branches.

The celebration lasted all day. Bands wandered through the crowds, playing loudly if not well. The bells kept ringing.

That night there was a fireworks display on the Commons. There had never been such fireworks in Boston. The air was filled with rockets, bright serpents, and spinning pinwheels. At eleven o'clock twenty-one rockets and sixteen dozen serpents were sent up all at once for a glorious finish.

A loud cheer went up for King George. Phillis wished that King George could know how happy the people were about what had been done. She wished someone would tell him.

After Phillis went to bed that night she tossed and turned. An idea was trying to form in her brain, but she was too tired to think about it. In the middle of the night the idea suddenly came to her—she would write to King George about how the colonists felt. Perhaps she could even write it in verse. She had written a poem not long before, but had not shown it to anyone.

She crept quietly out of bed and her candle burned for hours while she wrote. When she woke up in the morning she looked at what she had written. What a ridiculous idea, she thought. How could I ever have imagined that the king would read anything written by a young servant girl? She left the poem on the little table by her bed and almost forgot it.

A few weeks later Phillis was sick in bed with a cold. One morning Mrs. Wheatley brought a bowl of porridge for her breakfast. As she set the bowl on the little table, she noticed a scrap of paper there. She picked up the paper and asked, "What is this, Phillis?"

Phillis was embarrassed. "Oh, it's nothing, Mrs. Wheatley, nothing at all."

"But it is, Phillis. These are beautiful words. Did you copy this poem from a book?"

"Oh, no, Mrs. Wheatley. I wrote it myself, but it really isn't very good."

"You wrote it yourself? Phillis, this is remarkable. Why didn't you show it to us?"

"I was ashamed to show it to you, Mrs. Wheatley. I actually wrote it to send to the king, and then I decided that would be silly. Besides the poem isn't any good."

"May I show it to Mr. Wheatley?"

Phillis hesitated. Probably Mr. Wheatley would think the poem was foolish. But she said, "Yes, of course," and Mrs. Wheatley did not seem to notice her lack of enthusiasm.

That evening after supper the whole family came up to her room. Mr. Wheatley was holding the poem in his hand. He looked very solemn, and Phillis feared he was angry. Then he cleared his throat and said, "Mrs. Wheatley tells me you wrote this poem."

"Yes, sir," Phillis answered feebly.

"Now are you sure you really wrote it yourself? Sometimes we read something and don't remember it. Later we remember it but don't remember where we saw it. Then we may think we thought of it ourselves. Do you see what I mean, Phillis?"

"Yes, sir, I do," Phillis said, "But that isn't the way it was this time. I wanted somehow to make King George see how grateful we were. This was the only way I could think of. I know it was foolish of me, sir. I guess I was just excited over the celebration."

"I told you, Father," Mary said. "Phillis reads and reads and reads. She uses words I don't know how to use."

Mr. Wheatley cleared his throat again. "Well, then," he said, "in that case it's remarkable. Have you written any other poems?"

"Yes, sir. I wrote one about Harvard College. Would you like to see it?"

A few minutes later Mr. Wheatley left the room with both poems in his hand. Then one evening several days later he told Phillis that she was to go to the State House with him the next morning. "A few gentlemen there would like to ask you about your poems."

"They'll be angry," Phillis thought. "Mr. Wheatley shouldn't have told them."

Usually Phillis enjoyed looking at the gilded lion and unicorn over the State House door. Today she was too frightened even to look at them. Mr. Wheatley had told her that the most important men in Boston would talk with her.

Mr. Wheatley led her into the Council Chamber. Several stern-looking men who were seated at a long table looked up at her. Others looked down from gold frames on the wall.

"Stand at this end of the table where we can see you," one of the men said. He was holding her poems in his hand.

"Yes, sir," Phillis said in a low voice. She folded her cold hands in front of her to stop them from shaking.

"Mr. Wheatley tells us you wrote these poems," said one of the men.

"Yes, sir."

"Did anyone give you any help?"

"No, sir."

"Why did you write about Harvard College?"

"Because, sir, Mr. Nat brought back so much from

"Stand at this end of the table where we can see you," one of the men said. He was holding her poems in his hand.

there for Miss Mary and me to study and talk about. He even taught Latin to Miss Mary, and she taught it to me."

"Latin, eh?" a man said with interest. "Can you tell me what *E pluribus unum* means?"

Phillis smiled. "Yes, sir. It means 'one from many,'" she said.

Some of the other gentlemen asked questions in Latin which she was able to answer. They also asked her what books she liked to read. Then they began asking about her poems.

"Tell us what you meant by these lines, 'May each clime with equal gladness see/A monarch's smile can set his subjects free.'"

The speaker was Mr. Samuel Adams. Phillis had often seen him at the Wheatleys' house.

"I meant that we were glad the king used his power to make us happy. I'm sorry the meaning wasn't clear, sir," she said.

"I think it was quite clear."

The other gentlemen nodded. They asked her questions almost all morning.

At the end of the questioning, Mr. Adams smiled and said, "We shall send your poem to the king, and we hope that you will write many more. You have a great gift, young woman, a very great gift, and it must be used."

To The King's Most Excellent Majesty. 1768.

. . . But how shall we the British king reward?
Rule thou in peace, our father, and our lord!
Midst the remembrance of thy favors past,
The meanest peasants most admire the last.*
May George, beloved by all the nations round,
Live with heaven's choicest constant blessings
crowned!

*The Repeal of the Stamp Act

Chapter 8

Hard Times in America

"My thread's all tangled up again," Phillis sighed.

"Mine, too," Mary said.

Mrs. Wheatley was keeping her spinning wheel running smoothly. She and the girls were working in her big bedroom upstairs.

"I don't see how you manage to keep from breaking your thread," Mary said nervously. "Why did the king ever start all these silly taxes and cause so much trouble? As soon as he repealed the Stamp Tax, he began planning even worse taxes for us."

"He didn't know the taxes would cause quite so much trouble," her mother answered, stopping her spinning wheel. "He couldn't believe that the merchants here would agree to refuse to buy goods from England until the taxes were lifted. You know that the merchants are right, Mary."

"Of course they're right, but that doesn't make the

cloth any easier to spin or make us look any better."

"You shouldn't complain, Mary," Mrs. Wheatley said. "Your father never complains, even though he has almost no business left. Week after week he keeps hoping the taxes will be lifted and things will be better."

"Mr. Nat says some merchants aren't keeping their promise. They're buying materials from England and making money while the ones who refuse to buy are getting poorer."

"Nat is right, Phillis." Mrs. Wheatley's face was red. "And people who buy from those cheating merchants should be ashamed of themselves. They consider broadcloth and satin more important than their principles. I'd rather be poor forever than do something I didn't believe was right."

Phillis knew this was true. If Mr. Wheatley had been willing to buy materials from England, his tailoring shop would be busier than ever. Now all he had was the rough gray and brown homespun cloth which the colonists made.

Phillis saw many changes at the Wheatleys. The meals were plainer, and often there was no meat on the table. They burned the candles until they could be burned no more. They even melted the stubs to make other candles. Some of the Wheatleys' furniture was beginning to look shabby. They mended clothing to make it last longer.

One day Sophie ushered Mrs. Wentworth and Evelyn upstairs where Mrs. Wheatley and the girls were working. Mrs. Wentworth was wearing a smart blue dress and bonnet. Evelyn was dressed in dark green velvet.

"Are you people still spinning?" Mrs. Wentworth asked as she flounced into the room. She sat on the edge of a small chair by the fireplace. "I thought you'd given up spinning."

"We're not very good at it," Mary admitted, grimly trying to untangle her twisted thread, "but we haven't given it up."

"Why do you want to spin?" Evelyn asked, smoothing her already smooth skirt. "Homespun cloth is dull and ugly, and everybody buys material from England anyway."

"Not everybody." Mary looked down at her plain brown skirt.

There was an awkward silence. Then Mrs. Wheatley said, "The Harvard students are going to wear homespun cloth at their commencement this year. There may be much more spinning being done in the colonies than you think. Last month the Dudley family turned out four-hundred-and-eighty-seven yards of cloth and thirty-six pairs of stockings."

"And every yard uglier than the one before, no doubt," Mrs. Wentworth sniffed.

"Haven't you tried your hand at spinning even once, Isabel?" Mrs. Wheatley asked.

"No, I haven't. I think it's a silly, useless fad. What possible difference can it make to England whether we buy their material or run about looking like scarecrows?"

Phillis wished Mrs. Wheatley would lose her temper and tell Mrs. Wentworth what she thought of her. But Mrs. Wheatley only said, "John thinks it will make a great difference. Phillis, will you run down and tell Sophie we would like some tea?"

"Yes, tea would be good," Mrs. Wentworth said. "It's a cold day even for February. Are you ready to go downstairs?"

"No, we'll have our tea up here," Mrs. Wheatley said. "We don't keep a fire in the parlor in the daytime any more. It's a waste of wood since we spend much of our time up here."

Sophie came in with the tea. The big silver teapot shone as brightly as ever, but there were no little cakes on the tray. There was no dish of comfits or candied lemon peel. Instead, there was only a plate of thin bread-and-butter sandwiches.

"This should warm us up," Mrs. Wentworth said. She looked appreciatively at the steam rising from the thin china cup in her hand, but she took only a sip. "This isn't tea," she gasped. "What in the world is it?"

"Well, John won't buy regular tea as long as there's a tax on it." Mrs. Wheatley smiled. "This tea is made of dried raspberry leaves. We've grown quite accustomed to it, but I suppose it does taste rather strange the first time."

"Strange!" Evelyn exclaimed. "I think it tastes awful!"

No one said anything. Then the tall clock in the hall chimed. Mrs. Wheatley jumped up. "I'd completely lost track of the time," she said. "Phillis, you must get ready."

"I'd almost forgotten," Phillis said.

She ran to her room and changed her plain brown dress for a prettier gray one with white collar and cuffs. As she came back into the hall she heard Mrs. Wentworth say, "Susannah, I sent George back because Mr. Wentworth had work for him to do. I was sure you wouldn't mind letting Prince drive us home."

"Of course not," Mrs. Wheatley said, "but you'll have to wait until he takes Phillis to Mrs. Prentiss' party. It's almost in the opposite direction, and she's late."

"You look pretty as a jay bird," Prince said as he helped Phillis into the carriage. "I'm proud of you, Phillis. Sukey and Sophie are, too, even if they don't say so."

"Sukey maybe, but surely not Sophie," Phillis laughed. "Sophie and Mrs. Wentworth think the same about me. I'm a spoiled girl and a showoff, and no good will come of me."

Prince laughed. "Sophie's a little jealous maybe, but she wouldn't let anyone else say anything against you. You have a real gift, Phillis, and it's important for you to use it. Then folks will realize that it's what's inside that counts and not what's outside."

"That's what the Wheatleys think already," Phillis said.

"There aren't many like the Wheatleys," Prince replied, tucking a robe around Phillis.

On the way to the Prentiss house Phillis thought about what Prince had said. She had been with the Wheatleys seven years now, and she knew her good fortune. What if she'd been bought by some other New England family? She might even have been bought by the Wentworths or someone like them. She shivered and snuggled down further into the warm lap robe.

By now Phillis was well known in Boston and was widely invited to parties to read her poems. Some were afternoon parties, like this one, and others were dinner parties in the evening. Usually Mrs. Wheatley and Mary were invited, too, but they didn't always go.

"Phillis is our social lion," Mrs. Wheatley said proudly. "We don't even try to keep up with her anymore."

Soon the carriage drew up in front of a tall red brick house somewhat like the Wheatley house. Prince opened the door and ushered Phillis up the steps.

The owner, Mrs. Prentiss, stood in the doorway. "Phillis, I'm glad to see you," she said, taking Phillis' cold hand in hers.

Phillis looked at the women gathered in the parlor beyond the entrance hall. Most of them were dressed in gray or brown homespun. The few bright dresses in the room had been patched and mended many times. Mr. Prentiss was firmly against buying any materials from England, and no one dared come to his house wearing anything made from new British materials.

"We were afraid you weren't coming, and the party wouldn't have been complete without your new poem," Mrs. Prentiss said. "Let me have your cape."

Many people spoke warmly to Phillis as she entered the parlor. She forgot all about her cold hands and feet as she stood at one end of the room waiting to read. She hoped this was not showing off, but she couldn't help feeling excited when people listened to the words she had written. She thought this must be how mothers felt when people admired their children.

"Phillis has come, as you can see," Mrs. Prentiss said, "and I am going to ask her to read her new poem now."

Phillis began to read in her low, quiet voice.

Phillis began to read in her low, quiet voice, "Hail, happy day, when smiling like the morn, Fair freedom rose New England to adorn."

To the Right Honorable WILLIAM, Earl
  of DARTMOUTH, His Majesty's Principal
  Secretary of State for North-America. . .

HAIL, happy day, when, smiling like the morn,
Fair Freedom rose New-England to adorn:
The northern clime beneath her genial ray,
Dartmouth, congratulates thy blissful sway. . .

I, young in life, by seeming cruel fate
Was snatch'd from Afric's* fancy'd happy seat:
What pangs excruciating must molest,
What sorrows labour in my parent's breast?
Steel'd was that soul and by no misery mov'd
That from a father seiz'd his babe belov'd:
Such, such my case. And can I then but pray
Others may never feel tyrannic sway?

*Africa's

Chapter 9

"Town-born,
Turn Out!"

"Seven o'clock and all's well!" Phillis heard the deep voice of the night watchman boom out through the frosty air. She was riding through the snow in the comfortable sleigh with Mrs. Wheatley and Mary.

A large bearskin rug kept out most of the biting wind. It was the fifth of March, but snow a foot deep still lay on the ground.

Prince urged the bay horses to go faster, and their sleighbells jingled crisply. It was late for the ladies to be out. They had stayed much longer than they had planned at Mrs. Warren's house. The doctor had come home with exciting news just as they were ready to leave and everyone had stayed on to listen.

"The soldiers and the ropemakers had a serious set-to today," he had said.

"Was anyone hurt?" his wife asked anxiously, taking his coat.

"Yes, but none so badly that I couldn't put a bandage on him and send him home or to the barracks. There were mostly black eyes, bloody noses, and missing teeth."

"What caused the trouble?" Mrs. Warren asked her husband.

Dr. Warren sat down in his comfortable old chair. "One of the poorly paid English soldiers asked for work at Edward Gray's ropewalk. He needed the money, but some of the ropemakers argued with him. Then there was a fist fight and he ran away."

"He wasn't very brave," Mary commented.

"No;" Dr. Warren answered, "but he was very practical. He brought back eight soldiers, all armed with clubs and cutlasses."

"The soldiers swore they'd split some skulls," Dr. Warren went on. "The ropewalk men dared them and brought out tarpots and sticks. Finally they gave the redcoats a thrashing. I'm afraid the affair hasn't ended."

❖

Phillis worried as the sleigh glided smoothly along snowy Hanover Street. Would the soldiers and the townspeople be content to leave matters as they were? Mr. Adams hadn't thought so. And Mr. Nat had told her that the towns surrounding Boston had been warned that their help might be needed.

Suddenly Phillis saw the street came alive with men and boys running to and fro. Almost all of them were shouting.

"To the main guard!"

"Let's clean out the vipers' nest!"

"We'll give it to the lobsters!"

Suddenly Prince cracked his whip fiercely above the backs of the bays and urged them on. A man ran swiftly past them. His coat was flapping wildly and he had lost his hat. He called back over his shoulder. A crowd of soldiers followed with drawn swords.

"You're wrong and you know it. That makes cowards of you," the man panted.

"Catch him! Teach the dirty colonist a lesson!" the soldiers retorted. They ran clumsily in their red uniforms. Then one soldier yelled, "Let's stop running and ride!"

Prince shouted at the horses. They almost doubled their speed, and just in time. The closest soldier's fingers slipped off the side of the sleigh. Soon the horses drew up at the house. "Thank you, Prince. You saved us from a bad time," Mrs. Wheatley's voice trembled.

Prince smiled happily as he helped the ladies out of the sleigh. "I don't aim to carry soldiers around in Mr. Wheatley's sleigh, as long as these bays can still run," he said.

A man ran swiftly past them. His coat was flapping
wildly and he had lost his hat.

"Come, Mary and Phillis," Mrs. Wheatley said.
"Sukey will have dinner ready for us."

"Dr. Warren's story has taken my appetite away,"
Phillis admitted. "I wonder if Mr. Nat knows what
happened today."

"I'm sure he does," Mary replied. "In fact, I'm sure
he knows much about everything that's going on these
days."

"Do you mean because he belongs to the Sons of
Liberty?" Phillis asked.

"Yes, he goes to a meeting at the Green Dragon nearly every night."

❖

As they talked, loud shouting out on the street drew Phillis to the parlor windows. She peered out from behind the green damask drapes. In front of the house she could see ten or twelve young men. Most of them she knew. They were friends of Mr. Nat.

"I hope Mr. Wheatley comes home late tonight," Phillis murmured. "Then he won't see those boys with their heavy sticks."

Nat had been arguing a great deal with his father about his friends. Mr. Wheatley feared the hot-headed young men would get into trouble with the British soldiers.

Nat ran up the brick walk. "Don't be late tonight," she heard him call back over his shoulder. He pushed open the big front door. "How soon is dinner, Phillis?"

"As soon as your father comes home. Everything is ready." Then she asked softly, "Are the Sons of Liberty meeting tonight?"

"Yes, Phillis. We have much to discuss. The soldiers are becoming too quarrelsome."

Mr. Wheatley opened the door in time to hear Nat's

comment. "We should remember that our townspeople provoke much trouble," he said sternly. "Captain Preston has overlooked a great deal, but how much longer will he be able to keep his soldiers from striking back?"

"They're already fighting back, Mr. Wheatley," Phillis said. "Today down by the ropemakers there was trouble, and Dr. Warren thinks there will be more."

"Dinner is ready, sir," Sophie said, coming into the hall.

"Come, Father," Nat urged. "I'm starving."

"And eager to get back on the street again, I imagine," his father added dryly.

"Father, come to dinner," Mary called from the dining room. "Sukey's chicken and dumplings are getting cold."

"Very well, we are coming, Mary," Mr. Wheatley answered. In a lower tone he continued, "Nat, I beg of you, be cautious tonight. The temper of Boston is ready to be kindled by a single spark."

"I know, Father," Nat said soberly.

"You may be able to keep the wrong thing from happening. It is only for that reason that I permit you to join your friends tonight."

"I'll do my best, sir," Nat promised.

They sat down at the dinner table, but somehow no one was very hungry, even for chicken and dumplings.

"Father," Nat said as Sukey brought in the gingerbread, "did you hear that a sentinel at the guardbox hit the barber's apprentice with the end of his musket this evening?"

"Yes, I heard, but the apprentice had been teasing the sentinel," Mr. Wheatley replied. "Then he began to scream that the guard meant to kill him."

Outside there was a loud clamor from the bell in the Old South Church steeple. "I wonder why the bell is ringing," Mrs. Wheatley said.

The bell continued its clanging. Soon it was joined by the ringing of more church bells. Men ran out of their homes into the streets. Phillis listened carefully.

"Get the lobsters!"

"The sentry tried to kill the apprentice!"

Nat left the table. He opened the closet door and took his heavy coat from the hook. He wrapped a long wool scarf about his neck and started to leave.

His mother and father rose from the table. "Son—" Mr. Wheatley began.

"I must go, Father."

"I know you must." Mr. Wheatley's voice was husky. "And so must I." He put on his coat quickly. "This crowd sounds like a mob. There will be need for cool heads."

❖

"Town-born, turn out! Town-born, turn out!" came the cry. King Street had never been so noisy. Men and boys carrying lanterns and torches rushed toward the barracks. Nat and Mr. Wheatley joined them.

Mary and Mrs. Wheatley turned slowly back to the glowing fireplace in the parlor. Each busied herself with sewing. Phillis stood by the window and watched.

They sewed and waited, none knew how long. They moved only when the two men returned, long after the fire had died down to gray ashes and coals. "Here they come," Phillis said.

Mary and her mother stirred as if waking from a long sleep, and Mary ran to the door. When her father entered the house, she threw her arms around his neck and kissed him. "Oh, Father, we've been worried about you."

Phillis took the men's coats, hats, mufflers, and gloves and put them away. She noticed Nat's fever-bright eyes and Mr. Wheatley's white face. She knelt on the hearth to revive the coals. Soon a bright fire blazed, and she went to brew a pot of tea.

"Tell us what happened," Mary begged.

"It was terrible," Nat said. "The sentinel outside the Customs House had taken many insults from the gathering crowd."

"To say nothing of chunks of ice and oyster shells in snowballs," Mr. Wheatley added.

"Someone dared him to fire. He told everyone to stand back or he would." Nat's forehead began to look shiny in the light of the birch logs. "The moonlight was so bright we hardly needed lanterns," he went on. "We saw many men we knew. I've never seen such hatred and anger on people's faces."

"More and more people crowded into King Street," Mr. Wheatley put in. "The soldiers tried to push the civilians back."

"By that time the sentinel was hard pressed," Nat said. "Many were yelling, 'Kill the sentry.' Men in the back were pushing forward to see what was going on."

Mr. Wheatley took up the tale. "The sentry called for the guard. Captain Preston and seven of his men came running. Someone shouted for him to keep his men in order. 'They can't fire without my orders,' he replied. Cooler heads begged the people to go home, but some of the men at the back made a rush forward. Then all of a sudden a voice called out, 'Fire!'"

"Oh, no," Phillis moaned.

"I'm almost positive it wasn't Captain Preston's," Mr. Wheatley concluded.

"No, but it didn't matter," Nat said. "Crispus Attucks and one other man were killed instantly and two others were seriously injured."

"I thought I heard drums," Phillis said.

"You did," Mr. Wheatley answered. "The Twenty-Ninth Regiment marched into the street from Pudding Lane. The front rank knelt and the rear stood. Their guns were loaded. They were ready to fire."

"What stopped them?" Mary asked.

"Lieutenant-Governor Hutchinson spoke from the balcony of the State House," Nat answered. "He swore that justice would be done. He ordered the regiment back to the barracks. He told the mob to get off the streets and go home at once."

"And Captain Preston and his men have been arrested for murder and locked up in the Queen Street jail," Mr. Wheatley added.

The tale ended, the family went to bed. Phillis sighed. This had been one of the longest days she could remember. She could hardly drag her feet up the stairs. Certainly she would not write any poems that night.

A week later the sun was shining and the snow had melted. Phillis and Mary, thinking of spring and warm weather, walked to the market place around Faneuil Hall.

At the market place Phillis and Mary looked for a roast of beef, which Mr. Wheatley wanted for dinner. They approached heavy oak tables, where the farmers were cutting up quarters of beef and halves of pigs. An old man pushed a wheelbarrow of squirming lobsters.

In the distance the girls heard the roll of drums, but these were drums which were beaten by Boston citizens. The armed men patrolling the streets were colonists. The soldiers had been moved out of Boston.

"I'll be glad to think of something besides soldiers," Phillis said to Mary.

The British soldiers were finally brought to trial in the fall. It had taken a long time to find a lawyer to defend "these butchers," as they were being called. Josiah Quincy had finally agreed to defend them if John Adams would help him.

During the trial the soldiers were ably defended and fairly treated. Six were declared to be doing their duty and released. Two were branded lightly on the hand. Captain Preston was sent back to England. Phillis thought Boston could be proud that the trial was conducted so fairly for the soldiers.

Chapter 10

Ups and Downs
on the Ocean

"It's a good thing Miss Mary's wedding isn't till January," Phillis said, as she struggled to embroider a towel for her. She reached down to pick up her thimble and dropped her needle. Then she picked up the needle and pricked her finger. Soon a drop of blood spotted the once-white linen.

"I wish I could sew like Miss Mary," Phillis mourned. "I try hard, but I'm all thumbs."

Mrs. Wheatley patted her shoulder. "Many people can sew who can't write poems. At any rate, you're trying, and you'll have the towel finished before Mary's wedding."

Phillis sighed. She hadn't even started to write the poem she intended to write for Miss Mary. All at once she began to think of words that she might want to use. She stopped sewing and ran upstairs to start writing.

In the next few weeks she had to snatch whatever time she could to work on Miss Mary's poem. There were so many things to be done. She helped to sew endless rows of tiny black jet buttons on dresses. She helped Sukey stir up pounds and pounds of fruitcake. She helped Sophie clean the house from top to bottom.

Phillis hoped that by working hard she wouldn't think about missing Miss Mary after she was gone. Mary was going to marry a young minister by the name of John Lathrop. She would still live in Boston, but things would never be quite the same again.

Once more times were good. Most of the taxes had been lifted, and the colonists were happy and prosperous again. After the wedding, Phillis often stayed with the Lathrops for several days at a time. Then she turned to her books and writing for company.

More and more people were asking Phillis to write poems for special occasions. Apparently no birth, marriage, or death in Boston could take place without a poem by Phillis. She enjoyed writing and never turned down a request. Often she wrote until she was exhausted, her fingers were cramped, and she went to bed with a throbbing headache.

"You can't go on writing poems every time people ask you," Mary said one afternoon. "You're so thin, Phillis. I'm afraid you'll make yourself ill again."

"I like to write, Miss Mary. I don't know what I'd do if I couldn't write."

"I know you do, Phillis, but you're too unselfish." Mary smiled. "After what I've just said I almost hesitate to ask you to write a special poem for Mr. Lathrop and me. Do you remember the Reverend George Whitefield who came here from England last year?"

"Yes, I showed him some of my poems and he was very kind," Phillis said. "He even said they should be printed. Of course I know they weren't nearly good enough for printing, but it was good of him to say so."

"He was always very kind, Phillis, and he was a very good friend of my husband. Recently we were saddened to learn that he had died in England, a few months ago."

"Oh, I am sorry, Miss Mary."

"Now we were wondering whether you could find time to write a poem about him to send to his family and friends."

"Of course I will," Phillis answered. Already words were forming in her mind. "Happy saint," she thought. She must use those words. They described Mr. Whitefield so well. "Worlds unknown receive him from our sight," and perhaps "in Heaven's unmeasured height."

That night Phillis' candle burned long after everyone else had gone to sleep. Words came easily. There were so many things she wanted to say about Mr. Whitefield.

By 1773 Nat had married, and he and his wife were planning a trip to England. The Boston merchants were again buying goods from across the sea. However, they found that often they were being sent cheap goods which had not sold well in England. Mr. Wheatley thought that if Nat went to England he would be able to get better cloth for the tailoring shop.

In the meantime Phillis had become more and more exhausted and had kept on going to bed with splitting headaches. Often she laid down her pen almost as soon as she picked it up. Many of her poems were unfinished.

One day the Wheatleys had the doctor come to look at Phillis. He shook his head. "Possibly sea air and a change of climate would help her," he said.

Finally the Wheatleys decided that Phillis should accompany Nat and his wife to England. A few weeks before they were to sail, the Wheatleys called Phillis into the parlor. Mr. Wheatley handed her a sheet of paper. "Read this, Phillis," he said quietly.

"I, John Wheatley," Phillis began reading aloud. Then she stopped suddenly. This was a paper giving her her freedom. It was a generous thing for the Wheatleys to do, but Phillis had always felt free.

When she told them this, Mrs. Wheatley said, "You will always be part of our family, just as you are now, but we do not want you to go to England as a slave, even in name. Besides, Mr. Wheatley and I will not always be here, and you might need proof of your freedom."

At last Phillis stood on the deck of a sailing vessel which had just left Boston harbor. She admired the calm sea and the golden sunset which streaked the sky. She felt that she would be happy to have this voyage go on forever. Calmly she closed her eyes and listened to the sounds of the waves gently slapping the sides of the ship and the rigging creaking above her. The clean fresh breeze from the ocean blew away the last trace of the headache she'd had when she came on board.

She went down to the cabin to help Mrs. Nat, although there was little unpacking to do because there was no place to put things. She and Mrs. Nat would sleep in the ladies' cabin with other women passengers.

Phillis had barely reached the cabin when the gong rang for dinner. As she ate, she wondered how the cook had managed to prepare such a splendid dinner on board a ship. There were roast beef and duck, cabbage and potatoes, and a plum pudding. It had been a long time since she had been hungry, but now she ate everything which was put before her.

Once Phillis had curled up in her narrow upper bunk that night, she lay awake thinking how much she would enjoy a few months of this life. She had wondered if this voyage would remind her of the other long voyage she had made to America when she was a child. But her memory was dimmed by the years, and she couldn't feel unhappy tonight. She loved the gentle movement of the ship, back and forth and back and forth. Slowly she closed her eyes.

During the night she awoke. It was still dark in the cabin, and the gentle movement of the ship had changed to a savage shaking. The wind was howling, and there were mysterious bangings and thumpings from above the deck. Trunks were sliding noisily about.

❖

In the morning, the storm grew worse, and Phillis was seasick for several days, along with many of the passengers. When the storm was over, and the passengers were no longer seasick, many of them found the trip boring. The voyage went on day after day, and they became tired of looking at the sea and tired of looking at one another.

Phillis managed to entertain herself better than most passengers on board the ship. There were only a few books on board, and she read each of them several times. She had promised not to work on any poetry while she was gone, but she wrote long letters home. Just watching the spray break ahead of the bow of the boat fascinated her for hours. She spent much time watching the sailors climb the rigging or mend the sails.

Phillis was fascinated by the whales, sharks, dolphins, porpoises, and flying fish which were always to be seen. She especially loved the petrels which seemed to float slowly in the wind. Some of the men passengers tried to shoot the birds or porpoises while other passengers cheered them on. They would have been surprised if they could have read the thoughts of the slim brown girl who stood by the rail so quietly. "Please fly away," Phillis thought. "You're too beautiful to be shot."

There were days of dead calm when the ship barely moved. There were other days when the seas were so rough that the passengers took to their bunks because they couldn't stand up.

The closer they came to England the more Phillis wished she could go back to America with the ship instead of getting off. After she had written the poem about the Reverend Whitefield she had received a

Phillis was fascinated by the whales, sharks, dolphins, porpoises, and flying fish which were always to be seen.

flattering letter from the Countess of Huntington. Whitefield had been the chaplain for her household and had been very well liked.

When the countess learned that Phillis was coming

to England, she wrote that she would like to have the remarkable young poetess be her guest. She wanted to present her to English society, she said.

During the voyage Phillis hadn't thought much

about staying with the countess. Now that they had almost reached England, the very thought of being presented to society made her nervous. How would she be presented to society anyway? Would the important people wear crowns? What would she have to say to them? At times she almost hoped the ship would sink before she reached England.

A Farewell to America. To Mrs. S. W*.

I.

ADIEU, New-England's smiling meads,
  Adieu, the flowery plain:
I leave thine opening charms, O spring,
  And tempt the roaring main.

II.

In vain for me the flowers rise,
  And boast their gaudy pride,
While here beneath the northern skies
  I mourn for health denied...

*Susannah Wheatley

Chapter 11

By Phillis Wheatley

Phillis sneezed. It was almost the only thing she had been permitted to do for herself during the month she had been visiting the countess. She had thought the Wheatleys lived well, but she had found that the countess lived even better. There were servants to open the door and servants to arrange vases of flowers. There even were servants to help other servants. Phillis had a servant to help her dress.

Looking in the mirror now, she could hardly believe she was looking at herself. She had always worn her hair hidden under a little ruffled cap. Today it was combed with a single curl arranged to lie on one of her shoulders. The folds of a full-skirted pink brocaded dress swirled about her ankles. Her thin-soled slippers matched her dress.

As she stood there, the white-haired countess entered the room. "You look lovely," she said.

Phillis smiled happily. She had come to love this

sprightly little woman since staying with her. "How many guests will there be at the garden party this afternoon?" she asked.

"Surely not more than a hundred, although everyone is anxious to meet you since they have heard so much about you."

Phillis' smile faded. A hundred people! So far she had lived very quietly here. She and the countess had sat in the garden and talked. They had gone for drives in the carriage, or the countess had had a few friends in for tea. Phillis had enjoyed the guests before, but now the countess had insisted on giving a garden party in her honor. She musn't let the countess see how nervous she felt.

Each time Phillis saw the garden she enjoyed it as much as if she had never seen it before. There were flowers of every color. There were blue larkspurs and pansies, red coxcombs and zinnias, and roses on bushes, and little trees. Every bed was edged with primly trimmed dark green boxwood. Its sharp odor always made Phillis wrinkle up her nose.

Today, as Phillis stood by the countess in the garden, she failed to notice the color and fragrance of her surroundings. When the guests began to arrive, she was terrified. She didn't know what to say to these elegantly dressed people, many of whom were lords and ladies.

She realized that her face was stiff and that the countess was looking at her anxiously. She must smile and talk or the countess would be disappointed. Once she began thinking of the countess instead of herself, she felt more relaxed. At first she was afraid to raise her eyes, but now she began to look at people and to listen to what they said. Then she remembered that she had talked to some of the wittiest and most learned people in Boston.

For a time Phillis smiled and talked to please the countess. Then she realized that she really was enjoying herself. "Sit down and rest, Phillis," the countess urged her finally. "You've been standing all afternoon, and you look very hot and tired."

Phillis obediently sat down on a white marble bench. She was hot and tired, but now she could enjoy the sights and sounds of the party. Her bench was partly hidden by tall, dense shrubbery. She could listen to the chatter of guests without being seen. Many times she heard such remarks as "delightful party," "beautiful day," and "remarkable girl."

"I was very proud of you, Phillis," the countess said that evening. "Many people told me they enjoyed talking with you, but let's discuss something else. I have a wonderful surprise for you. It has been arranged for you to be presented to the king."

Phillis took a step backward. "Not King George?"

she asked faintly.

"Yes, King George." The countess smiled. "A member of the court remembered the poem you had written to the king upon the repeal of the Stamp Act. He felt that the king should meet you. It is a very great honor."

"Much too great for me," Phillis replied weakly. "I would like to please you, ma'am, but really I couldn't. I couldn't."

"Nonsense, child. It's all arranged, and tomorrow we'll start to make preparations. Your dress must be very beautiful and unusual, and I think I have an idea."

"When will I have to go?"

"You sound like a condemned prisoner, Phillis. It will be some weeks away."

In her heart, Phillis felt that it would be bad to be presented to the king, even if she still felt the way she had when she wrote the poem.

But now it would be worse, because she felt he had been wrong in his treatment of the colonists. What if her face showed how she felt about him? She was glad Mr. and Mrs. Nat had gone back to America.

The next morning the countess came in with some drawings. "I sat up most of the night working on these," she said excitedly. "You've told me many times how you enjoy the Book of Revelation. I've planned that your court dress shall be white satin embroidered with all the birds and beasts mentioned in the book. There are eagles and horses and lions. But what's the matter, child? I think it's a lovely idea. Don't you like it?"

"It is a lovely idea, ma'am, but why should I wear a dress like that and be presented to the King of England? I'm only a girl who has written a few rhymes."

The countess frowned. "You must realize, Phillis, that there are few men who write as you do, to say nothing of women or girls. Why, of course you must go. Now let's continue discussing the design. There are leopards and bears and serpents in Revelation, and I haven't even finished reading the book yet."

Phillis smiled and decided that there was no use in arguing.

The countess had also decided that Phillis must have her portrait painted. At first Phillis wanted to wear the beautiful dress which she had worn at the garden party for the portrait, but the countess wanted her to wear her usual plain clothes. "This is the way I want to remember you," the countess said, "and I have a special use for the picture."

Phillis was afraid to ask what the special use might be. She had thought she would be embarrassed to pose for the portrait, but she found herself looking forward to the mornings when the artist came.

He had her sit at a little desk which faced the long windows looking out on the garden. Sometimes she even forgot he was there, as she sat contentedly, warmed by the summer sun and amused by the antics of the countess' tiny French poodle, Pierre. The countess apologized for the hot summer, but Phillis had never felt so well before.

Usually after the artist had finished, Phillis spent the afternoon being fitted for her court dress. She had to stand very still for a long time. The full-skirted dress with its long train was heavy and hot. The dressmaker scolded, "Stand straight. Don't slump. You're making one shoulder higher than the other."

One afternoon the dressmaker warned, "We must finish our fittings soon. The countess insists that the dress be finished in three weeks."

Phillis felt cold in spite of the heavy dress. She knew that meant she would be presented to the king soon.

One afternoon the countess sent for Phillis to come to her sitting room. "I have a surprise for you, Phillis," she said. Phillis tried to look happy, but she couldn't help feeling a little nervous. The countess' surprises had a way of being overpowering.

Smiling, the countess held out her hand. In her hand was a small yet beautiful book. "Take it, my child," she said.

Obediently Phillis took the book. She opened it to the title page, but she could hardly believe what she saw! *Poems on Various Subjects* by Phillis Wheatley. Now Phillis remembered that some weeks before the countess had asked for copies of all her poems and had not given them back. Now she understood why.

Phillis couldn't say a word. Her eyes were filled with tears. If only the Wheatleys could be here at this moment, she thought. "I don't know how to thank you," she finally said. "This is something I never dreamed of."

"I've been so excited about it I could hardly keep from telling you," the countess said. "I took your poems to Mr. Archibald Bell, the publisher, almost as soon as you came. He was astonished at what you had done and said that he would be proud to print your book."

Phillis hoped that the countess would give her an opportunity to be alone with her book. Somehow the countess realized how she felt and said, "Take the book to your room, where you can look at it at your leisure."

Phillis tried not to run down the hall. She walked to her room, and she sat down in a small chair by the window. Then she opened the book and read, "By Phillis Wheatley." She ran her finger over the words as if she were afraid they would disappear.

She turned the first page. There was the portrait for which she had posed. To her delight, the face in the portrait looked much like the face she saw in the mirror each morning.

On the second page of the book there was a statement Mr. Wheatley had written after the gentlemen in Boston had questioned her about her poems. And in the rest of the book were her poems, page after page of them, neatly printed.

One day toward the last of September, a servant brought a letter from America. Phillis recognized Mary's neat handwriting. A month had passed since she'd heard from the Wheatleys.

She could scarcely wait to break the red wax which sealed the letter.

"Dearest Phillis," she read. "I do hope you are feeling better and that you are happy in England. Mr. Lathrop and the children are well and send you their love.

"I'm sorry to tell you that Mother is very ill. No matter what the doctor does, she seems to get worse. I spend as much time with her as I can, but the baby keeps me busy at home. We want you to stay in England until you feel absolutely well, but Mother's face surely would light up at the sight of you."

Phillis stopped reading and looked up without wanting to finish reading the rest of the letter.

She ran her finger over the words as if she were
afraid they would disappear.

Somehow she seemed to see Mrs. Wheatley's kind
face everywhere she looked. She thought of how Mrs.
Wheatley had looked when she knelt down to smile
into her face that first morning at the slave market.
She thought of the quick way Mrs. Wheatley always
defended her against Mrs. Wentworth's criticism. And
she thought of the many nights Mrs. Wheatley had

sat up to take care of her when she was ill.

A few days later Phillis stood in the front hall, her traveling cape about her shoulders, and a small satchel in her hand.

"I'm sorry about the court dress," she told the countess, who stood beside her. "Perhaps somebody else may be able to wear it."

"That dress is yours, Phillis, and I could never let anyone else wear it," the countess replied. "But it doesn't matter about the dress. What matters most is that you won't be presented to the king."

Phillis thought to herself that there were many reasons why she hated to leave England, but failing to meet the king was not one of them.

Chapter 12

Blankets and Feathers

Phillis looked up from her book. Outside the December evening was cold and windy, but it was warm and pleasant in the parlor by the fire. Mrs. Wheatley seemed better, and Mr. Wheatley was upstairs reading to her. Mr. Nat was home because Mrs. Nat was visiting her father in Bedford.

Suddenly the door burst open and Mr. Nat rushed into the hallway with two friends. They were talking noisily. "Shh!" Nat cautioned them. "I don't want to disturb my parents. I'm glad you're still up, Phillis. You can help us."

"I'll be happy to help you if I can." Phillis wondered why Nat and the others were excited. She knew there had been a meeting of the Sons of Liberty that day to talk about three ships from England loaded with tea. The colonists had refused to buy the tea because of taxes on the tea. They had begged the governor to send the ships away before there was trouble, but the governor had refused.

"There are a few Indian blankets in the attic," Nat said, "but we'll need some turkey feathers. Are there any feathers in the house?"

Phillis thought quickly and shook her head. "Only in the feather duster," she said.

"Pull some of them out," Nat ordered.

Phillis went to fetch it from the kitchen.

She couldn't light a candle because Sophie's room was next to the kitchen and Sophie was a light sleeper. She tiptoed into the pantry and reached for the feather duster, which hung on a hook. She tiptoed back to the parlor with the duster. Mr. Nat and his friends were already wrapped in the Indian blankets. One of Nat's friends began pulling out the big feathers, one by one.

"This bell pull will make good headbands," Nat said. Phillis held her breath as Nat took the embroidered bell pull from the wall by the fireplace and cut it into three pieces.

"Don't look so horrified, Phillis. It can be sewed back together again. Mother never uses it anyway." While Nat was talking he was tying the pieces around his friends' heads. Then he stuck three big feathers in each headband.

"Now, Phillis, can you get some ashes and rub them over our faces and hands?" asked Nat.

Phillis sighed and picked up a handful of ashes to

rub on the men's faces and hands. When she finished, the men looked almost like Indians in the dim candlelight.

"Now go to bed, Phillis," Nat said, "and don't worry. I may not be back for quite a while." The front door closed softly and the three Indians were gone.

Phillis sat in the dark parlor for a long time. It grew colder and colder. The clock in the hall struck eleven. Phillis shivered and stood up. There was no use in waiting any longer. Just as she reached the foot of the stairs the door opened very quietly and Nat slipped in. For a minute he stood with his back against the door, breathing hard.

"Are you all right?" Phillis whispered.

"Yes, I'm all right. Everything went well. Come into the parlor and I'll tell you what happened."

"Shall I light a candle?"

"It might be better not to. I don't think I was followed, but I might have been."

"Oh, Mr. Nat, what have you done?"

"Tonight, Phillis, I went to the biggest tea party ever held in Boston."

"Tea party?"

"Yes, since the governor wouldn't send the tea ships back to England, we boarded them and sent all the tea to the bottom of the bay."

"Oh, Mr. Nat, you'll surely be punished."

"Look at me," Nat laughed. "Would you have known me if you'd seen me on the street? And all ninety of us were dressed like Indians and couldn't be known."

"Was anyone hurt?" asked Phillis.

"No, Phillis, no one was hurt. We emptied three-hundred-and-forty-two chests of tea in three hours, and no harm was done to anything else. We broke one padlock but left money to have it replaced."

By now Nat and Phillis could hear voices in the street, and there was a thunderous knocking at the door. Nat ran toward the stairway.

"I'll go to bed," he said quickly. "Let Father answer the door. He thinks I've been here all evening, so he'll be convincing. I won't ask you to lie, Phillis, but act as stupid as you can, if you're questioned."

"Give me your blankets and feathers," Phillis said. She ran upstairs quickly and hid them under her mattress. Quickly she jumped into bed and pulled the covers up to her chin. She lay there, wide-awake and trembling.

Soon she heard Mr. Wheatley come grumbling down the hall. "It's getting harder and harder to get a decent night's sleep in Boston," she heard him say as he fumbled with the big bolt on the front door.

"We're officers of the Crown, and we wish to speak with your son Nathaniel," Phillis heard a loud voice say.

"My son Nathaniel has been in bed for many hours,

as all self-respecting persons have been," Mr. Wheatley replied calmly. "What is your business with him?"

"We have reason to believe that he took part in a crime against the Crown tonight," the voice answered sternly.

"How dare you, sir?" Mr. Wheatley sputtered.

"Will you call your son, or shall we look for him?" the soldiers persisted.

"I'll waken him," Mr. Wheatley said, "but this is nonsense. Will you be so good as to tell me what he is supposed to have done?"

"He helped to dump eighteen thousand pounds' worth of tea into Boston Harbor."

"Tea!" Phillis sat up in bed. What if some tea leaves had fallen from Nat's blanket when she ran upstairs with it? If these soldiers should find any tea, they would have proof that Nat was guilty.

She jumped out of bed, tidied her hair, lighted a candle, and started downstairs. She tried to look at each step as she came down, she couldn't look carefully enough without showing the officers that she was looking for something.

By now the three men had gone into the parlor. The officers were still explaining what had happened at the harbor.

"Who is that?" one of them asked as he saw Phillis. "She keeps late hours."

"This is Phillis, who takes care of my sick wife," Mr. Wheatley replied. "She is up much of the night, and my wife is too ill to be disturbed. If you have to carry on this ridiculous search, I'll appreciate it if you will proceed as quietly as possible."

"Come here, girl," the oldest man said. "Did you hear young Mr. Wheatley leave the house during the night?"

Phillis hesitated. "I've been in my room," she said, "except when I've been looking after Mrs. Wheatley. Now I've come down to get her some hot milk."

Mr. Wheatley looked at her sharply. This didn't sound like Phillis. Besides, when he'd left his wife, she had been sleeping soundly without any apparent need for milk.

As Phillis tried to smile at Mr. Wheatley, she saw something on the floor which made her catch her breath. Sticking out from under a chair was the end of the feather duster, with a few feathers left in it. She forced herself not to look at it. She must get the soldiers out of this room before they saw it.

"I think I hear Mr. Nat now," she said desperately. "You can ask him whether he went out." She went back into the hall, and the three men followed her. One of the officers almost stepped on the duster, but he didn't see it.

"You seem to be mistaken, young lady," the oldest

"Come here, girl," the oldest man said. "Did you hear young
Mr. Wheatley leave the house during the night?"

officer said and turned to Mr. Wheatley. "Will you
please get your son?"

Mr. Wheatley started upstairs and Phillis went
to the kitchen for the hot milk. When she came back
into the hall, Nat was just coming downstairs with
Mr. Wheatley. He almost convinced even her that he
had just awakened from a sound sleep. He had managed to scrub all the ashes from his hands and face.
His hair was mussed. He was yawning and wearing

a dressing gown over his nightshirt.

Nat could take care of himself, she was sure, but now she had thought of something else. One of the officers watched her as she went upstairs, so she tiptoed into Mrs. Wheatley's room. She left the glass of milk on the bureau without awakening Mrs. Wheatley.

Next she slipped quietly down the hall to Nat's room. There she discovered that Nat had thrown out the dirty water from his big china washbowl, but he had left a black sooty ring around the bowl. Quickly she took a white towel and wiped the bowl clean. Then she hurried back down the hall to her room and stuffed the dirty towel under the mattress with the blanket and feathers already there.

The officers searched Nat's room, and they looked carefully at the stairs. Apparently they, too, were looking for tea leaves, but they found nothing. They did not return to the parlor.

At last Phillis heard the oldest man say, "I must congratulate you on your cleverness. We find no evidence against you."

"I would take that as a compliment," Nat answered, "if there was evidence to be found, but I have done nothing wrong."

Phillis smiled. She knew that Nat really felt he had done nothing wrong. Whatever steps were needed to keep the colonies free were right and had to be taken.

Chapter 13

"First in Place and Honors"

The noise of the British troops' reveille floated through Phillis' open window. Usually she went back to sleep for a few minutes after it woke her up. Today, though, she was glad to wake up early, because she planned to go to the market to buy fresh vegetables. She wanted to go early in order to be there when the first farmers came to sell things. Quickly she jumped out of bed, dressed, and went downstairs.

Mrs. Wheatley had died the year before and Sukey had died several years earlier. Prince and Sophie had been freed. Now Mr. Wheatley and Phillis lived alone in the big house. Phillis did the cooking for Mr. Wheatley, but there wasn't much left to cook with.

The British had punished Boston for the tea party by closing its harbor. Now it was hard to find food even for two people sometimes. The other colonies had been very generous in sending meat and fish and flour and other supplies to Boston. However, no one could ever tell what foods would be available.

Mr. Wheatley was not well, and Phillis wanted to cook dishes that he liked. She knew he loved apple pan dowdy. She had enough flour in the pantry for the dough but needed to find some apples for the filling.

She carried a small basket over her arm, even though she really didn't think she would need it. As she left the house she stopped for a moment to enjoy the fresh fall morning. There was always something mysterious about the early morning before many people were stirring. She was the only person to be seen.

❖

Phillis saw many changes as she walked to the market. She felt especially sad as she passed the big stump where the Liberty Tree had been. The British soldiers had cut down the tree and used it for firewood. Perhaps they had also wanted to cut it down because it meant so much to the colonists.

Phillis thought about the happy morning when the people of Boston received news about the repeal of the Stamp Act only nine years earlier. They had decorated the tree with bright flags and streamers. Many things had happened since then, and to Phillis those nine years seemed almost like a lifetime.

She could hardly bear to look toward the Old South Meeting House where she had sat with the Wheatleys so many Sundays. The British officers had turned the lovely church into a riding school. They had poured tons of gravel over the floors to give a firmer footing for their horses, and they had used most of the hand-carved pews for kindling and firewood.

The market had changed, too. Instead of stalls loaded with plump chickens and geese and spicy sausages only two farmers were there with wagons to sell fruit and vegetables.

"Have you any apples to sell?" Phillis asked one of the farmers.

"Yes, I have," he answered, "but I'm sorry to say they're not very good. By the time the army takes what it wants, I haven't very many apples left to sell."

Phillis smiled. "I understand, but I'd like to see what you have."

Reluctantly the farmer dug down in his wagon and came up with a few wormy green apples. "I couldn't charge you for them," he said. "Take them along, and welcome."

All the way home Phillis thought of how she would surprise Mr. Wheatley at dinner with the apple pan dowdy. Her spirits dropped, however, when she entered the house and heard the voices of Mrs. Wentworth and Evelyn in the parlor. The only thing

"Have you any apples to sell?"
Phillis asked one of the farmers.

worse than a walk through Boston was a talk with the Wentworths.

Mr. Wentworth had died several years before, leaving Mrs. Wentworth and Evelyn their fine home, but little else. "It's cruel," Mrs. Wentworth was saying. "I couldn't believe the English soldiers would do this to us."

"An English officer stopped at our door this morning and said they would need our house," Evelyn added seriously.

"Did they refuse to let you stay?" Mr. Wheatley asked.

"Quite the contrary," Mrs. Wentworth said indignantly. "They asked us to stay and keep house for them. But I have never yet been a servant nor do I intend to be."

"That was shortsighted of you, ma'am. By staying you would be able to keep an eye on your possessions."

"That's out of the question, but I have another solution in mind. I thought of you and Phillis - living here alone."

Mr. Wheatley pretended not to hear her. "I understand no attempt is made to stop citizens from leaving Boston in any direction. Have you any relatives somewhere?"

"Only Aunt Martha," Evelyn answered. "And she

lives in a poky little house in New Bedford with no servants."

"The other solution I had in mind is this, Mr. Wheatley." Mrs. Wentworth did not give up easily. "Since only you and Phillis live here alone, you might like us to live with you."

Phillis almost dropped her basket. She was afraid Mr. Wheatley would give in, but much to her surprise he replied coldly, "No, madam. You chose to support neither the colonists nor the Crown, so you've ended up without having any friends anywhere. And, by thunder, madam, it serves you right."

"But what are we to do?"

"I would suggest that you begin looking for transportation to New Bedford."

Phillis shrank back into the dining room so she wouldn't need to speak to Mrs. Wentworth and Evelyn as they left. She almost felt sorry for them, but she knew Mr. Wheatley was right.

Phillis looked out the window as Mrs. Wentworth and Evelyn walked slowly down the street. She noticed that Evelyn still was wearing the same green velvet dress she had worn many months before. Now she and her mother were paying dearly for their imported dresses and East Indian tea. Most of their neighbors refused even to speak to them, so it was unlikely that anyone would take them in. How they would hate the little house in New Bedford. But Phillis felt even sorrier for old Aunt Martha than she did for the Wentworths.

Once Phillis was in the kitchen she began having trouble making the pan dowdy. She tried hard to cook the way Sukey and Sophie had cooked, but somehow she didn't have the knack. All she had to do was look at the fireplace and it started sending great puffs of black smoke out into the kitchen. Tonight was no different, and she wondered how a small fire could make so much smoke. She coughed and sneezed and moved the kettle of beans closer to the flames.

She struggled to peel the apples and make the dough for the dowdy. When the time came for dessert, Phillis was almost afraid to serve it. The apples were hard and the crust of the dowdy was soggy. Mr. Wheatley was so pleased with her attempt to make his favorite dessert, however, that tears came into his eyes. He insisted that it was the best pan dowdy he'd ever eaten, but Phillis knew that it was probably the worst. He even insisted on a second helping, and she hoped that he wouldn't suffer for his kindness.

Phillis went to bed shortly after supper. She couldn't sit in the parlor and read as she formerly had, because Mr. Wheatley was saving the small supply of firewood. Perhaps she would read in bed for a while before she put out her candle. She looked at her small shelf of books, each one of which meant so much to her. Finally she took down the small copy of *Paradise Lost*. This book had been given to her by Brook Watson, the Lord Mayor of London, on the day of the countess's garden party.

Two years had passed and now Phillis felt as if the garden-party Phillis was another girl. That Phillis, in her pink dress and slippers, had nothing more important to worry about than what she would say when she was presented to the king. This Phillis had many things to worry about—where to get enough food to cook, how to cook it, and how to take care of the big house by herself. She was worried because most of the time she was too tired to write.

By now a war had actually started with England. In April, 1775, the British soldiers had clashed with the patriots at Lexington and Concord. In July, a dreadful battle had been fought at Bunker Hill on the outskirts of Boston. In this battle the patriots had been defeated and driven from their position overlooking the city.

In early summer, 1775, the Second Continental Congress appointed George Washington to be Commander-in-Chief of the colonial forces.

His difficult job was to form an army of men who weren't soldiers at all. Instead, the men were farmers and blacksmiths and shoemakers. They had no real desire to fight, only to have a free country.

Suddenly Phillis felt ashamed for feeling sorry for herself. She was doing what she had to do, and her worries were small. George Washington was an important man who could have kept on working on his plantation. He could easily have refused to command the army. Instead he took this responsibility which he did not want, and his worries were great.

Before Phillis realized what she was doing, she was hunting for a scrap of paper. She had the excited feeling she always had before she began a poem. There were words and ideas waiting to be put down on paper, and she could hardly write fast enough.

"I shall call it 'His Excellency General Washington'," she thought. "And there are so many things I must say. 'First in place and honors.' 'Famed for thy valor, for thy virtues more.' 'Proceed, great chief, with virtue on thy side.' 'A crown, a mansion, and a throne that shine with gold unfading, Washington, be thine.'"

Phillis hadn't even noticed that as she wrote the darkness outside her window was changing to gray. By the time she stopped, the sun was coming up, but she was pleased with her poem. It said exactly what she felt, and she would send it to General Washington.

Chapter 14

"So This is the Poetess"

P hillis stared at the heavy sheet of paper in her hand. She read the bold signature "George Washington" at the end of the letter. Then she read the beginning words again to make sure the letter was really meant for her. Yes, there was her name.

With shaking hands, Phillis held the letter and started to read again, "Your favor of the 26th of October did not reach my hands till the middle of December. I thank you most sincerely for your polite notice of me in your elegant lines. The style and manner exhibit a striking proof of your poetical talents. If you should come to Cambridge or near headquarters, I shall be happy to see a person so favored by the Muses. I am, with great respect, your obedient humble servant, George Washington. Cambridge, February 28th, 1776."

A few months before, George Washington had come

to Massachusetts to help direct the colonial forces in the Boston area. His strategy was to turn the tide of the conflict and drive the British southward in the direction of New York.

Phillis was sure that she would never go to Cambridge to meet General Washington, but she would always treasure this letter. When Mr. Wheatley read the letter, however, he insisted that somehow Phillis must take advantage of the invitation. "This is an honor which comes to few people," he said. "You must go to see General Washington."

"I wouldn't know what to say to such an important person," Phillis said. "I would be afraid to talk."

"Nonsense, girl. You always say the right thing to everybody."

"I haven't anything suitable to wear."

"You look fine in what you're wearing now."

Phillis hoped that Miss Mary would support her refusal. But Miss Mary agreed with Mr. Wheatley. Still, it was several months before Phillis made the trip to Cambridge.

At last Phillis sat in a small room in Washington's headquarters. She felt very plain next to the officers in their bright blue uniforms with the shiny buttons. Suddenly she wondered what Mrs. Wentworth and Evelyn would say if they could see her waiting to speak to General Washington. Before she had time to

"So this is the poetess," he said.
"I had not realized you were so young."

worry any more, a young orderly ushered her into the
worry any more, a young orderly ushered her into the
room where General Washington sat.

The general stood as she entered the room. She
thought she had never seen such a tall man before.
"So this is the poetess," he said. "I had not realized
you were so young."

His smile and his voice seemed so warm that
Phillis was no longer nervous. She felt at ease and
talked freely, but realized that meeting this great
man would be one of the most important things which
would ever happen to her.

Later, Phillis received many honors for her poetry.
At the time when she lived, it was rare for a woman
to write either poetry or prose. For more than two
hundred years, she has been remembered as one of
the first American poets.

What Happened Next?

- In 1773, Phillis Wheatley's first and only book of poems was published.

- She married a free African-American man named John Peters in 1778.

- Phillis died in poverty in Boston, Massachusetts in 1784.

Fun Facts about Phillis Wheatley

- Phillis was the first African-American and the first slave to publish a book.

- Phllis was the first African-American woman to earn a living with her writing.

- She wrote her last known poem for George Washington.

- Phillis wrote more than 100 poems.

For more information and further reading about Phillis Wheatley, visit the **Young Patriots Series** website at www.patriapress.com

When Phillis Wheatley Lived

Date	Event
1753–1754	Phillis Wheatley was born in Africa.
1761	The Wheatleys purchased Phillis as a slave.
1765	Phillis Wheatley began writing poetry. The Stamp Act was passed.
1773	Phillis gained her freedom from slavery. The Boston Tea Party took place.
1774–1784	Phillis married John Peters, who was a lawyer, grocer, writer and speaker. The Revolutionary War started in 1775, and John Hancock signed the Declaration of Independence in 1776.
1784	Phillis died in Boston. The American colonies were free from England.

What Does That Mean?

bureau—low chest of drawers

comfit—kind of candy

apprentice—person learning a trade from a skilled worker.

mite—very small object or creature.

flounce—walk quickly in an angry manner

taffeta—shiny silk cloth

knack—ability to do something easily and well

petition—a formal request written to a person in power

About the Authors

Close friends from childhood on, Kathryn Kilby Borland and Helen Ross Speicher grew up in Indiana with backgrounds in journalism and newspaper editing. Over a 35-year career, they wrote 15 books for both children and adults, and collaborated on numerous reading texts for McGraw Hill and Scott-Foresman. The first edition of *Phillis Wheatley, Young Revolutionary Poet* appeared in 1968. Additional titles written by the two for the Childhood of Famous Americans Series™ include *Alan Pinkerton, Young Detective, Eugene Field, Young Poet,* and *Harry Houdini, Young Magician.*

Books in the Young Patriots Series

Watch for more **Young Patriots** Coming Soon
Visit www.patriapress.com for updates!

CPSIA information can be obtained
at www.ICGtesting.com
Printed in the USA
FFOW05n1926120815